SERPENT'S CURSE

Mark T. Bradbury

littlepondpublishing.com

SERPENT'S CURSE

By Mark T. Bradbury

Website address: mtbradbury1.blogspot.com

Copyright © 2013 by Mark T. Bradbury
ISBN: 978-1-940720-06-7
First Published 2013 Printed in the United States of America
First Printed 2013
Originally published by Little Pond Publishing, Inc
Cover Design by Naomi A. Mayhue
Book Production by Karen I. Smith

*Serpent's Curse is dedicated to the
men and women of the U.S. Coast Guard.
Thanks for all you do!*

PROLOGUE

Chichen Itza, Yucatan, 831 A.D.

MANY days and nights had passed since they had left the city, and his group had taken part in glorious celebrations in his honor throughout their lands. The priests and the nobles, his father among them, had taken him to all of the outlying villages to be feted by the local chiefs and tribal members. Everywhere they went the people of his land celebrated him for the part he would soon play in their destiny, because he was the anointed one, the one person who could save them from the devastating famine that had ravaged their land.

Nobody could even remember when the rains had come down from the Heavens, or when the Sun had not been so hot that it burned everything in its path. The Mayan farmers could barely grow anything from the dry, scorched earth, and food was becoming very scarce. Many of the wells had gone completely dry, and those that hadn't were getting lower by the day. Even the Sacred Well had dropped its water level, and none of the elders ever remembered that happening in their lifetimes. But because the water of the Sacred Well belonged to their benefactor, the Serpent God Kukulkan, they were forbidden by ancient decree to take that water.

Mother's breasts were drying up, and babies throughout the villages and cities were dying from the lack of their mother's milk. Older people were giving up what little food and water they had to their younger family members, and they, too, were dying in most unusual numbers. The priests of Chichen Itza knew that they had to do something soon before this period of death continued on its destructive path.

When the Ah Kin Mai (the High Priest) had asked his father to give up his oldest son so that the tribesmen across their lands would be saved, his father hadn't hesitated to grant the wishes of the High Priest. How could he? This was the highest honor a Maya could receive, and his boy would be immortalized as a true hero by his people. Now, after much traveling, they would return to Chichen Itza tomorrow, where his son's life would be celebrated one more time before his ultimate sacrifice.

Na-Chak Ha', son of Chak, a tribal noble of great heritage, would never be forgotten. He would rise in the morning for what would be a truly great event, bigger than anything else he had seen in his city during his fifteen years. Even his wedding ceremony, which had of course been cast aside, seemed to be nothing to him anymore. His chosen woman would be given to somebody else to bear children, and, thanks to him, the Mayan life would go on as it had for many hundreds of years.

But sleep was something that just wouldn't come to Na-Chak Ha'. He didn't understand why his father and the others had decided to camp for the night so close to Chichen Itza; it would have been good to sleep in his home with his mother and brother nearby, but the older men insisted that they camp here, just a short distance from their great city. He also wondered why everybody slept so close to him tonight, arranged in such a tight circle, almost surrounding him. Did they think that he might run away from this highest of commitments? He would never dishonor his father and his family, why would they think otherwise?

They would enter the city after first light, and begin the celebration then. The priests had told him that this would be a great day, and he knew that on this day, no Maya would miss the entourage's entrance into the city. No one would give up the chance to see the man who would save them all! Finally, exhausted, he drifted off to sleep, swept up in his own importance.

His father woke him just after the sun had made its appearance in the eastern sky. It was almost time to go; everybody in their party was ready to break camp and make the trek into their city. The men were eating maize cakes and bananas, but Na-Chak Ha' couldn't join them. He had been required to fast for the past three days, and because of the excitement, he really had no appetite at all this morning.

The men cleaned up their campsite and packed up their belongings. They filed out of the thick jungle into a clearing; this was where the Great Sacbes, the road into Chichen Itza, would take them the rest of the way through the gates and into the grounds below the temple of Kukulkan. Following the sacbes, the group entered the city in a short time. Na-Chak Ha' wasn't prepared for what happened when he entered his city. There were hundreds of people there from villages all over the Yucatan, the land of the Maya. He had never seen so many people here in his city, not even for the spring and fall celebrations to the Great Kukulkan, the *Serpent God*. They cheered him, a roar so loud that he thought his ears might explode! He was truly a hero to his people today!

Their procession went directly to the Temple of Kukulkan, a very large pyramid in the center of his city that rose into the sky. The temple was truly unique in its size and construction; twice a year the sun would cause the shadow of the Great Serpent himself to descend the stairs on two sides, eventually connecting the shadow body to carved stone heads of the God Kukulkan at the base of the temple. These were the holiest days of the year for the Mayas living inside the city's gates. It was said that Kukulkan visited no other place in all the land; this was his sacred ground, and the old city was the spiritual heart of the Mayan people.

The Ah Kin Mai and all of his other priests were dressed in their finest garments; in reds and greens, with lots of gold, and headdresses made with the wildly colored feathers of birds from the jungle outside the city gates. Na-Chak Ha' was humbled by the events, and began to feel like he was not worthy of this incredible celebration going on in his honor. He told his father of his feelings, but the man just squeezed his shoulder and told him that he was truly blessed. Then his father and the rest of his travelling party took their places on the lower steps, below the priests, leaving him alone before the steps of the temple.

The Ah Kin Mai welcomed him, and thanked him for his selflessness. Then the High Priest addressed the people of the Maya, and told them how important Na-Chak Ha' was to their survival. He went on to tell them that this was the holiest of days, holier than any other day in their ancient history. And he told them the ceremonies today would be unlike any others they had ever witnessed.

He began a series of incantations, and was joined by the other priests. Na-Chak Ha' was approached by four priests, or *chacs*, who began to strip him of his clothes. They placed an ornate headdress of gold and bright red feathers on his head, and began to paint his body blue. When they were done, the crowd roared again, and began to dance in the square below the temple.

As hundreds danced before him, Na-Chak Ha' began to feel that this was indeed the greatest day of his young life. Nothing could surpass the excitement he felt, and he realized that this must be how a God felt, for surely there could be nothing more exalted than this. While the chacs were getting him ready, Na-Chak Ha' hadn't seen the Ah Kin Mai and several of his priests climb the stairs to the chamber at the top of the pyramid. The revelry had continued, but as suddenly as it had started, the dancing stopped, and everyone was looking up at the High Priest.

The High Priest stood at the top of the temple, with his priests by his side. In his hands, and held over his head, was a large chain of gold, with a serpent's head that had eyes that burned even in the bright sunlight of the day. The Maya had never seen anything like this before; it was glowing like nothing earthly. The priests began a long chant, beseeching the Serpent God to come to their assistance. They begged him for his help; help that the Maya needed to survive. Please, would the Great God Kukulkan accept their offer and return the rains and bring cooling breezes to their stricken lands?

Na-Chak Ha' stood in awe at the temple steps. The Ah Kin Mai began the descent, with the others following close by. When he got to the bottom, and was face to face with Na-Chak Ha', he took the golden serpent chain and placed it around the boy's neck. The chain was so long that it needed to be wrapped around his neck several times before it was hanging with the serpent's head resting on his chest. The weight of the golden serpent almost brought him to his knees, but he saved himself from falling just as his father was about to assist him. The man looked down at his son, beaming with pride for the honor that the boy would bring his family forever. Nobody would ever forget his son and the sacrifice he made for them all.

The Ah Kin Mai told the Maya that this was the Serpent God Kukulkan, and that he had come down from Heaven to help his people. Pandemonium broke out on the field again, as the priests and Na-Chak Ha' began the ceremonial march to the Sacred Well. People cheered him as the parade made its way to the well, and he saw his family looking on as he approached the altar.

His mother, Ha', seemed to be very sad. He couldn't understand why she would be so sad; didn't she understand that he would be one of the few Mayas that would get to go to Heaven? Only the priests and the sacrificed entered Heaven; everyone else went to the Dark Place.

Why would she not be happy for him?

He faced the Ah Kin Mai, waiting for what would come next. Four other chacs picked him up and laid him on the stone altar above the well. The crowd grew very silent as the High Priest went through the ritual prayers of sacrifice. As he finished his prayers, the priest approached him, holding a ceremonial flint knife with a beautiful gold handle.

As Na-Chak Ha' glanced over at his mother, he suddenly felt the sharp blade of the knife cutting through his flesh. His body coiled, but the chacs held him down. He saw his mother again, crying now, and he understood why. As the pain raced through his body, the last thing he felt was the High Priest reaching into his chest and ripping his beating heart out!

His heart was offered to the Serpent God, and his blood was smeared all over the golden chain. Before his body could stop its involuntary convulsing, it was thrown into the Sacred Well, as a final offering. The Golden Chain of Kukulkan went into the bottomless pool with the boy, never to be seen again, or so the Maya thought.

CHAPTER 1

South Boston, Massachusetts – The Seventies

IT was coming at me fast and it was big; it was the size of one of Ma's corned beef briskets, maybe bigger, and it was closing fast. Bam! Lights out as they say; holy shit! It hit me harder than anything could possibly do, or so I thought at the time. I'd learn many times over how much it could keep hurting until I took care of stopping it myself, but I'll get to that later.

The brisket belonged to my father, '*Big John*' Burke, one of the meanest and toughest men in Boston. Many times I had heard my Ma crying and making awful noises in the bedroom after my father would come home from spending time with his mates at the Shamrock Café, but this night was different; it had gotten louder and rougher than I had ever heard before.

Big John, my dad, worked for the Irish Mob; he was the man that they had called on to break bones when somebody did something that the bosses didn't like. He was better at his job than anybody in town, and he quickly graduated from enforcing to being the boss of his own gang. He supposedly killed a couple of men along the way, but nobody could ever get a witness to testify against him. It was said that anyone who knew him, whether they were in the Irish or Italian mobs, or not, feared Big John more than anybody in Boston.

Big John liked to drink with his friends, and he came home drunk most nights. I had learned at an early age to hide when he came home; it wasn't smart to be around him when he was like that. My mother never learned that lesson, unfortunately, and she would get up in his swollen red face and chew him out for coming home like that again. Her reward for her trouble was usually getting shoved around, and mostly getting slapped hard on her mouth, something Big John seemed to take a lot of pleasure in. This was the *nightlife* for me in my early years.

But tonight was different; I was 13 years old, and I was about to challenge the man that was hurting my mother. I was mad, and I wasn't going to let him keep hurting her like that.

I came out of my room and banged on my parents' door. The noise stopped, and all I could hear was my Ma crying softly behind the door. My father asked me who it was that had the balls to interrupt his business, and I told him "it's me, Jackie; what are you doing to my mother?"

The door just about blew off its hinges and slammed the wall so loud that I probably jumped high enough to hit my head on the ceiling. It was then that I realized that I had made a serious mistake in judgment; the shit was about to hit every fan in Boston very soon, and I was the only thing in its way.

That's when I saw the brisket hurtling towards my face at warp speed; there wasn't any time to react. It caught up with my chin and I went down like a bag of potatoes. Stars, birds, whatever, I heard and saw them all as I lay sprawled across the hallway floor.

When I finally opened my eyes, my father was standing over me; his face was an ugly shade of red, twisted into a demonic snarl. He sneered at me and warned me with rancid breath to never get in his business again, because the next time it would be worse. It was at that moment that I was sure that my father, Big John Burke, was the Devil himself, and I had no reason to doubt his threats.

That was the first time my father had ever hit me with his closed fist; I had my share of slaps in the head, or across my *smart little Irish ass*, as he used to like to say when he was lighting my butt cheeks up, but I had never felt the real power of the man who was one of the most feared bad guys around. He was my dad, and I was John, Jr., the oldest of four kids, and in our house he was the king and nobody had ever questioned that until that night. It would be the first of many ass-whippings I got from him, because the more he hit me, the more I wanted to strike back. Pissing him off became my life's mission; it was all I ever thought about after that night.

CHAPTER 2

South of the Island of Coz-Mel, Yucatan February 15th, 1714

CAPTAIN Don Diego Montero stood on the deck of his ship, the Nuestra Senora de la Ascension. He and his men were assigned to guard the passages around Coz-Mel, an island off the coast of the Yucatan. The Spanish had a sizeable garrison there, and a small city had grown up around the fort. It was part of the Spanish protective line of defense throughout the Caribbean Sea; their military presence in these outposts was what had kept other countries out of their territories for many years.

Spain's war with the English and Dutch monarchies across the Continent was still very much a reality, and no Spanish captain could afford to drop his guard, since British privateers were everywhere in the Caribbean. They had been raiding and plundering Spanish galleons for several years, and had become very proficient at overcoming and capturing ships that had been unprepared. There were far too many former Spanish galleons that flew the flag of these men, so the Spanish Captains had become very wary of any ship approaching on the horizon. It was a dishonor to your King and your family to lose your ship to an enemy, but losing one to privateers was the worst sin of all.

Privateers! They were pirates, and he and his crew had strung up a few of these men before, watching them die for their sins. He wouldn't hesitate to do it again, either. This was the life he had chosen; to serve his King. The Spanish Navy had ruled the seas for two hundred years, and these damned British pirates weren't going to change that!

As he strode across the deck, he saw another ship sailing towards them. From up in the loft, his lookout yelled down that she was flying the Spanish flag. You could never be sure, since the pirates were known to fly the flag, only to drop it as they got close. By that time, it was too late, so careful planning was critical in these confrontations.

He told his executive officer to call all men on deck to battle stations. The word passed that this might be a pirate ship, so everyone was alert to that potential danger. As was the custom, the other ship had dropped its sails and slowed up, anchoring about a quarter mile away, out of cannon range. A longboat went over the side, and he saw a small crew start rowing towards his ship.

The men in the longboat identified themselves as being Spanish marines, and told the Captain that they had a message for him from the Admiral in Havana. They were allowed to board, and a young Lieutenant named Antonio Del Castilla stepped forward and saluted the Captain. He handed him a sealed letter, which the Captain took, and Captain Montero invited the Lieutenant into his cabin.

Before breaking the seal on the letter, the Captain learned that the other ship had just sailed from Havana, Cuba, a few days before. The Caribbean Fleet was based there, and the Admiral had dispatched the ship to Coz-Mel to give Captain Montero new orders.

The Admiral had gotten word from King Felipe' of Spain that hostilities across Europe might be coming to an end, and that he needed to raise money to pay off the huge debts he had built up with the banks there. The ships assigned to guard the Caribbean must now prepare to get the vast quantities of gold, silver, and jewels that had been piling up in Vera Cruz and Habana back to Spain. During the war, because of the combined threats of pirates and roving British warships, the treasure ships weren't able to leave 'Nova Espana', but everything must now be done to get that wealth to their King.

But the Captain's orders were quite different than he expected. The Admiral wanted him to take twenty of his most trusted men and go ashore in a place called Tulum, on the coast just south of Coz-Mel, where he would then turn his ship over to Lieutenant Del Castilla. He would be met there by an Army Captain named Don Pablo De Santiago. Captain Santiago would explain his orders at that time.

"What could this possibly mean? Why would the Admiral want me to give up my ship? I'm a Captain of the Royal Navy!"

"I'm sorry, Captain. I have no explanation for the Admiral's directive, since I was certainly not privy to his decisions. I was only told to give you your orders, and to take your ship to the mainland, so that you and your men may disembark. I know nothing more."

"I see, but I still don't understand; hopefully this Captain Santiago can explain to me what this is all about. We are very close to this place called Tulum; I'll have my first officer and the crew set a heading for that location, and we'll be off the coast of Tulum in a few hours. I will gather my twenty best marines, and be ready to go ashore to meet the Captain in the morning. My steward will show you to your quarters. Please take some time to get settled, and join me in my quarters for dinner later."

"Thank you, Captain. That is very generous. I will see you then."

The Lieutenant left the Captain's quarters, and was given a small room in the forward section below decks. He couldn't help wondering exactly what mission could be more important to the Captain than that of Master of his ship, but he knew that as a faithful servant of the King, the Captain would of course follow his orders. And then he, Antonio Del Castilla, grandson of the legendary Captain-General Don Pedro Del Castilla, a hero of the Spanish Armada, could move into the Captain's quarters; this was the opportunity that he'd been awaiting for several years.

CHAPTER 3

Sebastian, Florida
September 25th, 2004

THE two men stood behind the bar of the old watering hole. The wind outside was howling with an intensity that was worse than that other pain in the ass, Frances. Hurricane Frances had come through the East Coast only two weeks before, and nobody was ready for another catastrophe like that again. "Why do they always make these damned hurricane names sound so friggin' good?" CJ asked. This one was called Jeanne.

"Jesus! Jeanne! Sounds like somebody I wanted to do back in high school for Christ sakes! Why don't they call 'em *'Ball Buster'* or *'Shithead'* or sumpin' like that? Don't make no sense it's so stupid!"

"Hey Ray! I think they should name one after you, man. They could call it *'Numbnuts'* and everybody on the whole East Coast of Florida would know it was named after you!"

"Up yours, asshole! You got any more weed, man? I'm startin' to lose my high, ya know?"

"Yeah, I got some, but if this damned Jeanne don't

go away pretty soon, we're gonna have to go out and try to track down a new stash."

"Yeah, right! Why don't you go ahead and get a head start, man? I'll just stay here and make sure the friggin' roof don't blow off this place. Shit, this is nasty! It's really gonna mess up the fishin' out there now. We probably won't catch no fish 'til Christmas, the way it's going."

"Shit Ray, you ain't caught a decent fish for months anyhow."

"Yeah, like I said before; up yours, asshole!"

Ray Eldridge and CJ Hilton were two of Sebastian's finest. Not cops, but drunks and potheads. They were part of the original cast around town; their families had shown up four generations ago to work the farms, and they'd been there ever since. Not that Ray and CJ worked much. When they weren't smoking dope or getting drunk, they were out fishing. And most of the time that they were fishing they were drunk or high anyhow. Fishing was supposed to be their job, but most everybody knew that they made very little money at it, and what they did make, they quickly pissed away.

But life was good for these two. They had played football and baseball in high school, and they had partied in between. It had been twenty years since they managed to graduate from Vero Beach High School. Not even their mothers thought they had enough sense to get a diploma, but they got one anyhow. Class of '84. You go Indians!

But now they were just two local rednecks, with little or nothing to offer except an occasional sarcastic remark. They mostly amused each other, their friends said. Hell, nobody else could understand them half the time, and that's when they were straight!

Ray's Uncle Bob had bettered himself more than most of the Eldridges around town. He had worked hard, and saved up enough to put down a deposit on a little bar down Route 1 just north of Wabasso. He called the place *The Scales & Bones Pub,* an effort on his part to attract all the local fishermen and bikers. He had a local artist draw up a logo for his sign out front. It was a mullet driving a Harley, what else? He thought that this would really bring'em in.

All it did was attract his nephew and CJ, with all their loser buddies. But he loved his nephew like a son, since his wife had given him four girls. (What a trip she was!) He gave Ray a job tending bar three nights a week so he could get some time off to spend with his newest girlfriend. Some folks said his girlfriend looked just like the mullet on the bike, but she seemed to make him smile most of the time. You know what they say about 'ugly women', right?

When Ray worked, his Uncle Bob knew that things might not go so well. Ray didn't give a damn if somebody wanted to fight or throw things around. He was usually too high to notice, but what the hell; he was blood, and you put up with your family.

That's how Ray and CJ ended up in the Scales & Bones Pub the night that Hurricane Jeanne hit. Everybody else had been smart enough to go home before the storm moved in, but these boys didn't usually get mentioned in the same sentence as 'smart'. Things got more interesting as the night wore on, and the storm kept coming.

CHAPTER 4

Tulum, Yucatan
February 16th, 1714

Just before dawn, three longboats left the Nuestra Senora de la Ascension. The Captain and his men had packed provisions for several weeks, as they had been directed, and set off for the ancient Mayan seaside city of Tulum. Captain Santiago had set up a camp on the site, and was waiting there for them with their new assignments. There was a soft beachhead sandwiched between two natural rock cliffs where they could land the boats, and as they approached the beach they saw a group of men waiting for them.

Aside from the welcoming party, the Captain couldn't see much activity coming from the old city, just a few small campfires left over from the night before. He had sailed past this site many times, but always well offshore. As he got closer, he couldn't help but marvel at the Mayan temples perched on the cliffs above the beach. These buildings had been built by the savages that had inhabited them several hundred years before, and they were very impressive in their design and structure. It was said that this was one of the only seaside cities that the Mayans had built, and the local legend was that it had been the last of the great Mayan cities.

When the Spaniards under Don Francisco Hernandez de Cordoba had first landed here in the Yucatan in 1517, they had sailed their way down the coast from the north, where they had originally landed on an island they named *Isla de Mujeres,* or Island of Women, named so because of the stone statues of the Mayan Goddesses they discovered. Finding some small amounts of gold there, they continued their exploration southerly to the island of Coz-Mel, where they found Mayan ruins, but no gold. Sailing along the coast, they discovered former Mayan settlements at Xel-Ha and in this city of Tulum. Still no gold, but stranger yet, there were no people living at any of the Mayan sites. It had seemed to them then in their recollections that the native Indians had literally disappeared sometime before they had arrived. But the stone work that these Mayans had created was quite extraordinary, and stood today as it may have for hundreds of years.

As the longboats approached the beach, the Captain saw a small group of soldiers and some Indians awaiting them. He knew that the Spaniards had employed the Indians since their initial settlements two hundred years before, but he had also been told that many of the local Indians resented the Spaniards, and weren't to be trusted.

Decades of unrest between the Indians and the Spanish soldiers had come to a head many years before, when the Catholic Padres had won over the local tribes, and trouble flared up between the priests and the men seeking their fortunes in New Spain. Although the soldiers had felt that victory was theirs, the Priests were the ones that had won the hearts of the Indians, and they had become the most powerful group in the Yucatan. It was said that if you wanted to work with the local Indians, then you had to have the approval of the priests; he wondered if the padres were in favor of this mission; even though he didn't know what he was about to do, he thought that it would certainly be better with the help of the Lord. It was still a wild place here.

As the rowers launched themselves on a crashing wave, the boats hit the sandy beach with a jolt, and many of the men lost their seats. Captain Diego Montero held his stance, not willing to show these strangers any weakness, lest it would weaken his position with them. He chuckled softly to himself. *"Position? What position?"* He didn't have the slightest clue what he and his men were doing here, or whether he still had a 'position', but he would soon learn his fate.

Captain Don Pablo de Santiago stood in front of the group on the beach. He was a large man, certainly fit to be an officer in the King's Army, and he had an air of authority, even though he was clad only in breeches and a light tunic. He wore no hat, and he was very dark, almost as dark as some of the Indians accompanying him. He had obviously spent some time outdoors here in the Yucatan, and he seemed very comfortable in this steamy climate.

"Welcome to Tulum, Captain Montero! We have been looking forward to your arrival for days." He reached out to help the Captain as he jumped off of the boat.

"Thank you, Captain Santiago! Although I'm not sure why we're here, I welcome the opportunity to see this ancient city so close up. I've admired it from afar on several occasions. It is quite remarkable."

"Yes Captain, it is. It's actually a very strategic spot along the coast here, and must have been quite a vibrant port in its time."

"Does anybody know how old this city is? Or why there's nobody living here anymore?"

"No sir, but the local Indians talk about the city as being the homeland of their ancestors. They say that no one has lived here for over three hundred years, but you can still almost feel them here in all of their temples."

"Are you saying that you can feel their ghosts, Captain?"

"I guess that I wouldn't say that, at least not out loud! But come; let me show you the city."

There was a break in the stone cliffs overlooking the beach, and the group made its way up through the opening. As they reached the top of the hill, the city spread out below them. There were buildings everywhere. Some were almost completely intact; others were only stone foundations. There was a series of streets throughout the site, and the wall that surrounded the city was quite impressive. The wall was approximately 8-10 feet high in most places, higher in some. In the northwest corner and the southwest corner there were stone watchtowers built into the expanse. The fortifications were definitely an architectural wonder of unknown age.

"Captain Santiago, I'm overwhelmed by the elaborate work done here by savages. They obviously took great pains to build this city. It's very impressive!"

"I agree Captain. I had the same reaction the day I landed here. Why don't I show you to your temporary quarters, and then we'll sit down to discuss our mission."

"Temporary? Are we not staying here?"

"No sir, we'll leave in the morning to begin our adventure. But come, let's get you and your men settled, then we'll have some breakfast."

"Very well, Captain Santiago. I must confess to wanting to know what it is the Admiral has in store for us."

"I will fill you in soon, Captain. But you should know that this task is not for the Admiral, but for King Felipe' himself!"

CHAPTER 5

Breakfast

CAPTAIN Montero and his men settled into one of the old stone buildings in the center of the city. It was said by the local Indians that this had been the *castle* of the King, with all of the small side rooms being chambers for his many wives and children. It wasn't much of a castle, at least not like the castles he had come to know in his native Spain, but this old place certainly seemed to be the largest of any of the dwellings in this part of the city, and it had a freshwater well right outside in the courtyard.

Looking around at some of the other buildings nearby, he noticed what appeared to be a two-storied temple of some sort. On each corner of the building there was an ornate carving in the stone that seemed to be a large head. The *heads* were painted with some sort of red paint or dye, and the effect was quite interesting. "These savages were indeed quite a talented bunch," he thought.

When their gear was unloaded, they went back up towards the cliff to meet with Captain Santiago and his men for breakfast. The Captain's headquarters stood on top of a stone floor. It appeared that the posts and roof beams were recently cut, and the roof was thatched with palm leaves. There were no walls, and only a few rough hewn tables and benches. Captain Montero wondered to himself how long the Captain and his men had been here waiting for him and his crew. "And what in God's name were they here for?"

Captain Santiago rose as the group approached the hut. "Welcome again, Captain! Let's eat, and then we'll discuss our mission. I'm sure you'd like to know what's going on."

"Thank you, Captain! You're right! I was just wondering to myself when I might find out."

"Well then, let's not delay. Let's go to my quarters and have the men bring us something. It will be much more private there. Please, follow me."

The two men walked a short distance from the large hut to another very unique stone building. This one also had two floors, but the Captain was only using the lower space. Again, he couldn't stop thinking about the talents that these Mayan builders possessed; it seemed strange to refer to them as savages once you had seen their incredible architecture.

Sensing this, Captain Santiago remarked that "I'm sure that once we get to see some of the other things that we shall see in the next few weeks it will only amaze us more! It is said by the locals that this city was built more for protection than as a cultural center, but where we will be going is very different than this. I personally am very excited about our upcoming trip!"

"Then please, Captain, tell me where we're going, and what we'll be doing."

"Certainly! I'm sure that I would be crawling out of my skin to find out, so I don't blame you for being impatient. Please sit down, and I'll tell you why we're here."

"I have been chosen for this mission by King Felipe' himself. My oldest brother is a noble of very high rank in the King's Court. The King and my brother are old friends, and my brother is one of the King's most trusted allies. It is for this reason that I stand before you; my brother and the King expect me to do nothing less than complete the task before us.

About a year ago, I was ordered by King Felipe' to explore the Yucatan, in the hope of discovering gold for the King's treasury. Although other parties had been unsuccessful over the years, the stories that kept coming from the locals indicated that there were some very sacred sites in the interior that had yet to be discovered.

Before starting inland, we camped in Xel-Ha, a few miles up the beach. It was said that Xel-Ha had been an important Mayan site, and that there was a strong possibility that we would discover something there. There were underground springs and cenotes, deep pools that seemed to have no bottom, scattered throughout the region. Legend has it that many of these cenotes were used by the Mayans for human sacrifice, and that offerings to their gods had been thrown into these pools.

I had my men recruit local Indians to dive the cenotes and springs to search for lost relics. However, after several weeks, we had found nothing more than an underground river that seemed to come from the rocks themselves. We found no gold or treasure.

The only treasures that Xel-Ha had to offer were

thousands of beautiful fish that came in from the ocean each day. In frustration, I had my men pack up our gear and shut down our camp.

We came here to Tulum next. Thinking that this might be a potential location for gold, we set up this camp. Again, we hired local tribesmen to help us dive and explore the cliffs. We had them swim at the base of the cliffs, thinking that there might be a secret cavern somewhere. We dug up the dirt floors of some of the temples and other buildings, and still found nothing. This, too, seemed to be a waste of time.

So we moved on again. I next went to a small site named Muyil, a two day's march from here. It proved to be another false hope. But one of our Indians told us about a very large city not too far from there, a placed called Coba. He promised us that this place might hold the treasures we were seeking, and that it was only a day to the west of where we were.

We set out at first light. After marching all day, we were suddenly attacked by a sizeable force of Indians, which we eventually turned away. But, not expecting an attack, I lost twenty-seven men to the savages, and I had to return to Tulum; the Indian guide who was with me said that we were a very short distance from Coba when we were attacked.

I requested aid from the garrison commander on the island of Coz-Mel, but the Commandant could spare no men. As I'm sure that you're aware of, he had been having frequent skirmishes with British Privateers, and he was already undermanned. I returned to Havana on the next ship that I could get to meet with the Governor and the Admiral.

Unfortunately, they too were under regular attack from the British and Dutch Navies, as well as having the pirates attacking their vessels far too often. I wasn't able to tell them everything about my mission, but I did have a letter from the King instructing anyone I met with to assist me with my duties. And this, Captain, is where you come in."

"But why me and my crew? We are Royal Navy, not Army."

"That's true, but you have the finest reputation of any Captain in the Caribbean Fleet, and it is said that your marines are the fiercest, most dedicated fighters on any of our ships. That is why you and your men are here, Captain; to help me find the treasures that our King needs so desperately."

"Well, I certainly appreciate the respect and confidence bestowed upon me by the Admiral. I will do whatever I can to make your mission a success!"

"I never doubted for a minute that you would respond any differently, Captain. It is my honor to serve you."

"To serve me? I thought that this was your mission."

"No, Captain, you are the ranking officer here, and it shall be you who leads us to riches. I will serve as your executive officer, and I would ask that my two sergeants be placed in charge of all of the men, sir. They have been with me since our first excursion here."

"I see no problem with that, Captain. My men will be informed of the new rankings immediately. Expect no problems; they will follow us to the death if necessary.

Are these Indians part of our expedition? And if they are, can we trust them?"

"I believe that we can trust them. Most of them were with me when we were attacked in Coba, and two of their friends were killed by the attackers. The new ones are all family members of the others, so I think that we'll be fine with them."

"Then when shall we set out, and where is our first destination?"

"I still believe that Coba may hold some treasure. Why else would the locals attack us, if they weren't defending something of value?"

"Then Coba shall be our first stop. We'll set out at first light. Pass the word to your men, Captain. And let's be sure that we're ready for any attack this time!"

CHAPTER 6

Sebastian, Florida
September 25th, 2004

A T about ten o'clock the power had gone out at the Scales & Bones Pub. The battery powered radio that Ray's Uncle Bob kept under the bar for emergencies was squawking noise that could barely be understood above the howling wind and the slashing rain that pelted the old place. Ray had enough sense to find the kerosene lanterns out back before the power went down, so he and CJ were quite comfy. They had plenty of beer (even though it was getting warmer since the power went down), and they still had enough *ganja* to get them through the night.

"You know Ray, this ain't half bad. Shit, we got everything we need here. I think this is a great place to be right now."

"I got to tell ya, CJ, it is pretty damn nice in here, ain't it? All we need is a couple of good looking sluts, and some fried chicken, and I'd think we died and went to Heaven, man."

"Hell Ray, them sluts wouldn't even have to be good looking, would they?" They both laughed so hard they almost pissed their jeans. "And I don't give two good shits about that fried chicken; man we got enough pretzels and beer nuts to live for months!"

"Yeah man! You're right. What was I thinking?"

The radio barked under the bar. "They're talking about the *Eye Wall* coming at us sometime in the next hour. What's that shit all about?"

Ray reached under the bar and put the radio on top. He fiddled with the dial until the station cleared up a bit. They listened for a couple of minutes, and decided that no Eye Wall was gonna scare them. They were here for the duration.

"CJ, why don't you get us another beer, and bring me some of those beer nuts, will ya? You made me hungry talking about them little devils."

"Yeah, alright, but how about rollin' another joint, dude? I think it's time we fired one up."

"Shit man, when don't you think it's time to smoke one?"

As they both laughed at their own jokes for a few more minutes, they didn't notice that the storm had intensified. The old bar seemed to be creaking, like it was going to explode. The rain had become so heavy that the entire parking lot outside was under water. The storm drains weren't able to handle rain like that, and soon Route 1 would be impassable, but they were having too much fun to notice.

Until they heard a roar that sounded like a freight train coming through the living room, they didn't have a clue; but that noise woke them up.

"Holy shit, man! What the hell was that? It sounds

like the train's coming!"

"I'm not sure, CJ, but I remember somebody saying one time that's what a tornado sounds like before it hits. I think we better get our asses under the bar, quick man!"

"Are you shittin' me, dude? This ain't Kansas, Dorothy. Shut the hell up and roll us a bone, man."

"I'm not takin' any chances man. Get your ass down here and pray that this ain't what I think it is! And you better do it now!"

"Man, I didn't know my best friend was some kind of sissy. What's the matter, Sally, got your panties in a wad?"

"CJ Hilton, you can kiss my sorry ass on the steps of St. Sebastian's if we live through this, but I'm covering up now!"

As Ray ducked under the bar, the building groaned. The wind had become unbelievable, and it must have been doing 150, if it was moving at all. The freak noises coming from the old building caused CJ to give up his bravado, and he moved under the bar with his friend; the timing couldn't have been better. They heard a howl like no other just before the east side of the building collapsed.

As soon as the wind had an opening, it ripped through the bar like a demon from Hell. The boys were prone on the floor behind the bar when the front doors blew out and onto US 1. Chairs and tables were tossed like toys, and the rain soaked everything in the place. Just when they thought that things couldn't get any worse, the roof fell in on them, knocking them both out.

It was not a good night at the Scales & Bones Pub. In

fact, after the storm had cleared it was determined pretty quickly that the Pub would never reopen at this location. There was nothing left but the Cypress slab bar that Bob Eldridge had built himself.

They found Ray and CJ the next day. Ray's truck was still out back in over a foot of water. Bob knew that they must have tried to ride out the storm at the bar. He got some friends to help with a front end loader, and lifted the old roof off of the bar. There they were, on the floor, out cold, sleeping like a couple of babies.

CHAPTER 7

South Boston, Massachusetts

I COULDN'T stay out of trouble no matter what. I was the oldest son of an Irish Catholic family from South Boston, and like every other Irish kid in Southie, I was sent off to the Catholic school, where I was supposed to be trained by the Sisters and Priests to grow up to be a fine upstanding young Catholic man. There was only one problem with this idea, though; I was Big John Burke's boy, and nobody was going to train me to do anything that I didn't want to do.

I went to St. Margaret's for eight years, and hated most of it. The Sisters and Priests weren't quite as nice as they were supposed to be; I had felt the Sister's pointer across my knuckles many times, and one of the Priests loved to take his belt to my naked ass. After eight years, I had enough of the 'Catholic way of life', as the nuns liked to call it.

I convinced my parents to let me go to South Boston High School, the public school in town. I quickly discovered that to get by in this school a boy needed to be tough. The teachers there didn't give a damn about the kids; there were too many of us, so they didn't watch over the students like the nuns did. I began to get into fights with some of the Italian boys, and even with some of the other Irish. The boys of South Boston High School learned quickly that Jackie Burke wasn't someone to push around, unless you were looking to get your ass kicked. Big John had nothing on me!

At the end of my Junior year I was called into the Principal's Office; my Guidance Counselor and the Principal were waiting for me. They read off my three year list of infractions; fourteen suspensions for fighting, one for painting graffiti on the Stadium wall, and literally hundreds of detentions. I was asked not to come back in the Fall; they didn't want me, and thought it would be best for all if I just moved on with my life, as if I knew what the Hell that meant.

I disappeared for a while after that, and came home pretty late. The school had called and talked to my Ma. She had told my father, and Big John was waiting for me. He was pretty drunk and pissed off, and I was already madder than hell about what had happened at school. After enduring his shoves and slaps for a few minutes, I made the decision to strike back. With my fists closed, I started swinging at my old man; I let years of anger flow out of my body. My father, shocked by my actions, tried to fight back, but I was too young and strong for a drunken forty-five year old. I hit him with every ounce of power in my body until he started to realize that I wasn't 'little Jackie' anymore; I was beating the shit out of him and loving every second of it! My father went down on the carpet, and he didn't get up.

On my Ma's good advice, I left home that night, and moved in with the older brother of a friend from school. I started looking for a job, but there wasn't much for a seventeen-year old kid to do around Southie, so I started hanging out with my roommate and his crew. The older boys were into several things, none of them legal, and I started learning *the ways of the street,* as the boys liked to call it.

We ran numbers for the Irish bookies, sold some recreational drugs, and group *breaking & enterings* became weekly events. I became the star of the team, and took over the gang within six months. There was nobody tough enough to challenge me, because, like my father, I had become a very large and mean man. But I always seemed to come up with new ways to make some easy money, so life was good for our crew. I had my own little band of merry men before I was eighteen. Everyone in town said that it was only a matter of time before I made Big John look like an altar boy at Easter Mass.

CHAPTER 8

The Road to Coba, Yucatan
February 17th, 1714

As the men packed their gear for the march ahead, the sun broke through over the top of the cliffs. It was a hot sun here in this land, and the Captain's marines would have to get used to it quickly. There would be no sea breezes to cool them down, and no chance to jump out of the longboat for a cooling swim. Here, on land, the air got very humid and very stifling, so maintaining a steady pace was essential. Having enough water to drink was equally as important, but they were told that there were cenotes along the route to replenish their supplies.

The Indians led the way for the soldiers. This was their homeland, and they knew the easiest route to Coba. The group marched for several hours, and then stopped for a rest and a meal. Captain Santiago had explained that it was necessary to their survival to make sure that their men stayed fresh and ready to fight, should they encounter hostiles again.

"Part of the reason that we were ambushed the last time, Captain, was that I was led to believe that there were no hostiles in this region. I pushed my men too hard, and when we were attacked, the men just didn't have the strength. That's why I feel that we need to proceed more cautiously, and rest the men regularly. Living in this heat is hard enough, but trying to respond to an ambush when you're tired and thirsty is more than our men can handle. The Indians here have lived their entire lives in this wretched heat, and don't seem to be affected by it all."

"I understand, Captain. What you say makes sense. I'll defer to you when we take our breaks; let me know when you think the men need to stop."

"I will, sir. But for now, I think that we should resume our pace, and make camp before nightfall. I remember a rocky ledge a few hours from here. I think that we should make our camp there, and have the high ground in case of problems."

They arrived at the spot that the Captain had spoken of and set up camp for the night. Sentries were posted around the top of the ledge, and were changed out during the night. They encountered no problems, however, and they broke camp after having breakfast.

Along the way, they saw Indians, but none that seemed to pose a threat. Most were older men and women, or young women with children. The guides explained to them that the men were probably tending their crops of maize and cacao, and were very busy. The growing season here in the Yucatan was only a short period of several months, and it was critical to the survival of these Indians that they harvested their crops before the sun became too hot to grow anything.

About mid-afternoon, Captain Montero saw that

the road changed from packed dry dirt to field stones laid in a pattern, like the streets of Sevilla, in his native land. "Are these roads the work of the Indians?"

"Yes, Captain. The Indians told us that these roads, called 'sacbes' by the locals, are part of a network of paved roads that the Mayans constructed in and around their major cities and ceremonial sites. In Coba, it is said that there are over fifty sacbes, going out in all directions. They're really quite fantastic!"

"They certainly are. I was thinking that they remind me of home in Sevilla."

"Yes, they do look a lot like the streets of our native Spain in some ways, but the surrounding jungle reminds us quickly that we are in a very foreign land. We should be in Coba before dark, unless we run into my old friends. I remember seeing these paved roads a short time before the attack. I think that we should stop here and send some advance scouts ahead to see if we have any company awaiting us. I pray to God and the Virgin that we have a peaceful arrival."

"Yes, Captain, I hope that you're right. I'm anxious to begin our little adventure."

CHAPTER 9

Phu Quoc Island, Vietnam
August 28th, 1971

ENSIGN Rick Perry, USCG, sat at the beachside bar staring out at the sun setting in the western sky. Phu Quoc was one of the most beautiful places he had ever been, and the sunsets there were arguably some of the best he'd ever seen. But this wasn't some 'Spring Break' week like he'd had in college, and he didn't have his surfboard waxed up and waiting for the next big curl. No, this was Vietnam, and there was a whole lot of trouble going on all around him. He finished his beer and left to get some sleep; the days here came early.

His father had been a Coast Guard *lifer*, spending over twenty-five years in the Coast Guard. Rick had grown up wherever his dad's service took him to. San Diego, California, was where he learned to surf, and New London, Connecticut, was where he became hooked on fishing for saltwater striped bass and bluefish every summer. Long Island Sound offered the best surfing and angling combination in the Northeast, so he had grown to love the area even more than San Diego. It was during this time that he had become a die-hard Boston Red Sox and Bruins fan; baseball and hockey had become a huge part of his teenage years, so New England was now his favorite place to be.

He went to Southeastern Massachusetts University in Dartmouth, Massachusetts. The city of New Bedford was nearby, and it had long been a maritime center. Whaling and the *China Trade* had made it one of the most active seaports in New England during the 1800's, and the plethora of local seafood had brought Portuguese settlers from the Azores Islands to the city in the 1900's. The local captains found that the Portuguese immigrants were great fishermen, and they worked harder at it than any of them had ever seen, so the New Bedford fishing fleets became a home for hundreds of these men. Those who couldn't find jobs on the boats were able to land jobs in the local textile mills, and over the years the Portuguese immigrants gradually became a large majority in the city.

Because of the extensive maritime activity, the Coast Guard had a large station on the waterfront. Only Boston's, to the north, was bigger than the New Bedford base. They had formed an alliance with the local college over the years, and had a very active ROTC program there.

Rick Perry was drawn to the program *'like a moth to a flame'* as they say; he enrolled as a young freshman, and stayed in the program until his graduation just a few months ago. He had hoped for duty somewhere in New England, since he had adopted the region as his home, but there was a rather large skirmish going on in Southeast Asia back then, something called the *Vietnam War.*

Ensign Rick Perry, formerly of Connecticut, found himself on Phu Quoc Island at the bottom of the Mekong Delta. He was in command of a Coast Guard rescue boat running the river every day, assisting in the evacuation of wounded or picking up stray troops that had been separated from their units. The island offered their boats and helos sanctuary from the craziness just upriver, so it had been a perfect place to set up their command center.

When they left the beauty and tranquility of Phu Quoc every morning and headed northwest up the Mekong, they knew that they might not come back. Their boats were constantly fired on by Viet Cong insurgents, locals who were loyal to Ho Chi Minh, the Communist leader of North Vietnam. It was impossible to guess where they might attack, since they seemed to come out of thin air before attacking and disappear just as quickly. In his short stint here in the Mekong, Rick had seen a couple dozen body bags of Coast Guardsmen come back to his base. The helos would fly them up to Saigon, where they would be sent home for full ceremonial honors.

He had a strong desire to fly the helicopters, but that job was one of the most dangerous options in Vietnam. The North Vietnamese Army was supplying the Viet Cong with RPG's, rocket-propelled grenades, and the Cong had become very adept at blowing choppers out of the sky. Perhaps he'd wait until he got back Stateside to apply for Helicopter Training School; if he ever got out of here at all.

CHAPTER 10

Coba, Yucatan
February 19th, 1714

"Captain Santiago, tell me about Coba. Is there anything that you learned from your last trip there?"

"No sir. We never got close enough, but the Indians who are with us have said that it is a magnificent place, unlike what we've seen at Tulum and Muyil. They say that some of the buildings there are very large, and that one reaches into the sky. At Muyil, there's a large temple that reaches perhaps four stories high. We named it the *Castillo*, since it is quite impressive and reminded us of castles back home. But the Indians claim that it cannot match the temples at Coba."

"Then I'm looking forward to seeing this city. Perhaps you are correct in thinking that there may be treasure here. It appears to be a very important place."

A few minutes later, one of the scouts ran back to the party. He approached the Captain and said "Sir, we see no sign of hostiles anywhere. We found our way into this city, and it is the most incredible place. You will not believe what you will see."

"Then, Captain Santiago, let's move on into the city now, before dark, and set up our camp. Tell the men to be ready for anything, though. I don't want to be surprised like your last group."

"Yes, sir, I will tell them."

They arrived at the city about an hour later. This site was huge, spreading out in every direction. There were hundreds, maybe thousands, of buildings here. Some were fully exposed, and some had been covered over with vines and trees, but the Spaniards could easily see that this was a very large settlement.

"There could be Indians anywhere in here, Captain. How would we know? I don't think that our men could possibly secure this site, given the size of it", said Captain Montero. "What do you recommend?"

"Well sir, I think that we should find a large building that is a little separated from the rest. We can make our quarters there, and secure the perimeter."

"It will be dark soon. I think your idea has merit, so let's find a building that will accommodate us, and secure it immediately."

They were following one of the sacbes, and this particular road had spread to at least thirty feet across. It seemed to be leading them into the heart of the old city, so they stayed on it, hoping to find the right encampment soon. What they saw next was something they weren't prepared for.

There was a temple in the middle of a large square that actually did seem to reach into the sky. Surrounded by several smaller pyramids, it was close to one hundred and fifty feet high, and a set of steps led up the front of this pyramid to what looked like a small chamber room that must have been the main altar room. It was a visually stunning edifice, even larger than what the Indians had told them on the way here. The Indians told them that the pyramid was called 'Nohoc Mul', and what they thought had been exaggeration turned to a stark reality; the Mayans were truly an advanced civilization.

After recovering from the surprise of the large pyramid, they surveyed the rest of the square. Buildings of different shapes and sizes surrounded them. There were other pyramids, large multi-storied square units and long flat-roofed stone buildings. There were carvings on the stones, much more elaborate than what they had seen at Tulum.

They picked one of the long rectangular buildings as a base, and sent the men to secure the location. It was up high; not as high as the pyramids, but high enough to defend if they were attacked. Stone steps led up all four sides, but well placed sentinels could see any problems that might arise.

There was a very large open room, accessible by two doors, one on each side of the building. The men were told to use this room as general quarters. Captains Montero and Santiago found two smaller anterooms to use as their personal quarters. Sentries were assigned around the temple, and the men prepared a meal before night fell on the city.

The Indians slept outside on the stone terrace, not wanting to stay inside the temple. They knew that they had brought the Spaniards here, and some of the ancients might not be very happy that they did so. To a man, they felt that being out in the open was the wiser choice.

For the fortunate men inside, sleep came quickly. The two days march to Coba had been difficult for them. They weren't used to the oppressive heat, and it slowed them down more than they'd like to admit. Most of them prayed to the Virgin, and thanked her for their safe journey, and asked for her blessing, as they continued their mission. They also prayed that the Indians outside weren't right about the 'ancient spirits of the Maya'.

CHAPTER 11

Coba, Yucatan
February 20th, 1714

As the sun started to peak through the forest that surrounded the city, the men inside the temple started waking up. They were refreshed, and ready to start this 'adventure', as the Captains liked to call it. They had been briefed before they left Tulum about their mission. They knew that many men had died near here during the last expedition, and some of them, who had been with Captain Santiago, had gotten wounded in that skirmish. Everyone knew that this could be a very dangerous place.

One of the sentinels rushed into Captain Montero's quarters. "Sir, the Indians are all gone. We never saw them leaving, but there are none of them here at the temple."

"You fools! How could two dozen Indians sneak away without one of you seeing them?"

"I don't know, Captain. We never heard or saw a thing out of the ordinary. They must have left just before dawn. They had been there all night."

"Well, soldier, you and your sleepy-headed friends out there will be the first ones called upon for the manual labor that certainly awaits us. Get out of here!"

"Yes sir. I'm sorry sir!"

"Captain Santiago, what do you think about this unexpected setback? What are we to do now?"

"I'm not sure, sir. I think that…"

"Captain Montero, come quickly! To the front of the temple; hurry!" cried one of the men.

Not believing that one of his men would address him that way, Captain Montero went out onto the terrace. What he saw then made him understand the marine's insolence. The temple seemed to be surrounded by Indians in every direction. There were hundreds of them! "My God, what next?" he thought.

After the initial shock wore off, he started to evaluate the situation. There were more Indians here than at any other place he had been before, but they didn't appear to be hostile. There were women and children, young men and older men, but nobody was saying or doing anything. What could this be about? And did he need to worry?

Captain Santiago and his sergeants had gotten their men into defensive positions around the temple. But forty men couldn't be expected to hold off this crowd if violence was their plan. His marines were the best in the Caribbean Fleet, but the numbers were indeed overwhelming, and he really didn't think that they could last long with these odds. So he decided to wait them out; to see if anyone took a position, or made an attempt to speak to them. His patience was rewarded when an elderly Indian man came forward to speak.

In somewhat recognizable Spanish, the old Indian

asked the Captain why his men were here. "Did they wish to harm the sacred ground of his ancestors?" he asked.

Captain Montero stepped forward. It had been apparent to everyone that the old Indian had been speaking directly to him. He now knew where *their Indians* had gone to early this morning. This man must be a tribal chieftain, and he must have spent a lot of time with the Catholic priests, who taught their language to only the most important tribal members.

"I am Captain Don Diego Montero, and I am in charge here. We wish you no harm; we only wish to explore this ancient city, to marvel at its richness, so that we might tell others of this beautiful place."

"I have been told that you are here for gold and treasure, Captain. Is this not so?"

"Chief, I'm sure that you know that the Spanish people have been here for two hundred years, and I'm sure that you can understand that the King of Spain owns these lands and any riches that might be here. I am here to claim the King's right."

"Our ancestors have lived on this land for thousands of years. The buildings around you have been here for hundreds of years, some longer than that. The ancient gods gave my people this land, and no King has ever owned it. We covet no treasure; our treasure is our land and our freedom. You can take the gold and other riches, but leave my people to live on our own like we have for centuries."

"Then could you help us find this gold you speak of, so that we might bring it to our King in his honor?"

"You will find no gold here. The treasures you seek

have left Coba long ago. Only its' people remain."

"We hear from your people about legends of gold and other riches. If they are not here, then where are they?"

"Most have disappeared over the centuries. You are not the first to seek gold in our land. The Toltec's first came here looking for the same thing. They took most of everything that was valuable here three hundred years ago."

"Then are you telling me that no treasure exists in the Yucatan? That there is no place that we might find it here in all of your land?"

"There is one place, a place so sacred that even the Toltec's wouldn't go near it. It is possible that you might find what you're looking for in this place. But I can't promise you that you'll live to take it home to your King."

"Where is this place? And what do I need to fear?"

"This place is the sacred city of Chichen Itza. It is three days to this city from here, if you follow the sacbes in the northeast corner of the city. Chichen Itza was the most sacred of places for the Maya, and it is said that hundreds of people were sacrificed to the gods in this holy place. It is there that you need to go; go to the Sacred Well, east of the Temple of Kukulcan, the Serpent God. You will recognize his temple by the serpent heads at the base of the temple's steps. Follow the sacbes to the Well. You may find treasure there, although I can't be sure."

"And what is it that I must fear, Chief? Are there men who would die to defend this place?"

"The souls of the Dead defend the Sacred Well. No Indian will go near that place for fear of offending the spirits that dwell there."

"Will you allow our Indians that deserted us this morning to continue with us to this city? I need their assistance in getting our provisions there, and I'll need them to work at the site. Can they do this?"

"They can do whatever they wish, but none of them will go near the Sacred Well. They will accompany you to the city, and help you set up camp, but they will not help you recover anything that might lie at the bottom of that unearthly pool."

"That's better than no help at all. Thank you, Chief. I will take your word as truth and leave Coba today."

"May your God help you Captain. Adios!"

With that, the old chief turned and walked away from the temple. His people followed him, until there were just the men who had left camp before dawn.

Captain Montero waited until the last of the Indians had disappeared into the city. He summoned his men to the front of the temple and said "We must leave immediately. Get your gear and provisions ready as soon as possible; we'll leave within the hour. Captain, see to it that our Indian friends understand what we expect from them for the remainder of this expedition. We can't afford to lose their help again. Let's go men! Everybody get moving!"

CHAPTER 12

Sebastian, Florida
September 31st, 2004

A LMOST a week had passed since Hurricane Jeanne
had destroyed the East Coast of Florida. Sebastian
was part of what the Chambers of Commerce in the region liked to call *'The Treasure Coast'*, but its' waterfront,
once so quaint and picturesque, still looked like a bomb
had dropped there. The remains of boats that had torn
loose from their docks littered the shallows of the Indian
River. Homes and businesses along Indian River Drive
were damaged severely, and others were completely destroyed. Docks along the river were torn up, with whole
sections of commercial dockage disappearing.

The storm hadn't just touched the shoreline of the
beaches and the riverfront, but had cut a large path
through most of the interior sections for miles. Jeanne
had come ashore south of Sebastian, in Stuart, in the
same spot that Hurricane Frances had come through just
two weeks before. This was amazing in itself, because the
Treasure Coast hadn't had a bad hurricane hit it since
Hurricane Dora in 1964, and then had two severe cy-

clones land in the same place just two weeks apart. The overall damage was devastating to the entire coast. The beaches suffered major erosion damage and flooding of lowlands. The storms had shifted sandbars and reefs to totally new places, and navigating the Indian River or trying to get out of the Sebastian Inlet to the ocean became a very serious challenge. The Coast Guard had asked everyone to keep their boats, if they still had one, off the water for a few weeks, to give The Army Corps of Engineers a chance to free the Intracoastal Waterway of debris. The Inlet channel, they warned, had shifted, and it, too, needed to be cleared.

It was not a good time to be a fisherman in Sebastian.

CHAPTER 13

Chelsea, Massachusetts

ONE of the new money makers for my crew was *carjacking.* I had hooked up with a Puerto Rican guy from Dorchester who ran a *chop shop*, and my new friend introduced us to the very lucrative field of demand and supply. Diego would call me to tell me what he needed, and the crew would go out and steal what he wanted. It was a perfect deal, and the money was flowing like never before.

Diego had gotten in touch with me and told me he needed Jeep Cherokees; they were so popular around Boston that finding them wasn't hard at all. We went to Chelsea, just west of the Produce Markets, and stationed ourselves in an alley adjacent to a very busy intersection. It was after nine, and it was raining; it was a light drizzle, but enough to keep most people home that night. Cars were few and far between, and an hour went by before we saw a Jeep coming up on the light. It was perfect; nobody else was in sight.

We walked out into the street right in front of the car. Tim Hogan, the idiot of our group, loved to smash the windows out. He had his crowbar out, and went to the driver's side window. As he swung the bar, we heard a shot coming from the car. Tim staggered backwards, clutching his chest. He reached into his jacket, took out his gun, and started shooting wildly into the front seat of the Jeep. As Tim went down on the street, I told Pat Whelan to get the car. As Pat wheeled up, we heard sirens coming fast; we loaded Tim into the car, and headed down the street.

We got about a quarter mile when we were blocked by two Boston Police cruisers. The cops were standing outside with their guns drawn, and as I thought about what to do, more police came up behind us. It was over; we had no place to go. One of the policemen called out on a bullhorn for us to get out of the car, hands up, and lie down on the street. Not having much of a choice, the crew did what we'd been told.

I couldn't help wondering why the hell these cops were here so close to our job. It had seemed like they were on top of us before we even got in the car. I started to sense that they might have had a little help from a friend, somebody who knew our routine, and where we were working that night. It was all too coincidental.

After being handcuffed and thrown into several squad cars, we were brought Downtown to Central Booking, where we were finger printed, and had our photos taken. It was now *official*; me and the boys were real criminals, with ink stained fingers, and mug shots for everyone. And we were definitely in a shitpot of trouble!

CHAPTER 14

Chichen Itza, Yucatan
February 23rd, 1714

THE expedition arrived outside Chichen Itza late in the afternoon of the third day, as the old chief had promised. It would be dark soon, so the decision was made to set up a camp for the night, and to enter the city in the morning. As the Chief had told them, no Indians would go near the Sacred Well, but they might lie in wait inside the city's temples. It was best to wait.

At dawn, the group moved into Chichen Itza. Captain Santiago had sent scouts out during the night, anticipating trouble, and hoped to avoid a disaster. The men had come back a short while before, and had reported that they had seen nothing inside the city. Everything appeared to be right for their entrance into the city.

Captain Montero had the men spread out across the sacbes leading into the square. There was something about this place that made him feel uneasy, and he didn't want to get caught off guard, as had happened in Coba. The Concepcion's marines led the way; they fanned out in a large V shaped formation, and proceeded with caution.

The Captain knew that if there was trouble ahead, that he and Captain Santiago could count on them to a man, so he let them lead, and Captain Santiago's troops followed up the rear. The Indians from Coba stayed well behind the men; they felt the eyes of the spirits of Chichen Itza watching them, and they didn't want to be anywhere near these soldiers if something were to happen.

As the men continued into the center of the city, they began to see temples on either side of them. But to their right arose a large pyramid, with a chamber at the top. It was very much like Nohoc Mul in Coba, but it wasn't as high. Steps appeared to ascend the temple on all four sides, and at the bottom of the eastern and western facing stairs were the carved stone heads of the serpent, as had been described by the old chieftain in Coba.

This was the Temple of Kukulcan, the Serpent God. The men stood in awe of the temple. Although not as tall as the Coba pyramid, this monument was the most imposing edifice in the city. It dwarfed the other temples around it, and its shadow darkened many of the other buildings to the west.

There was no sign of hostile forces anywhere, or at least nothing that could be seen. Captain Montero suggested to Captain Santiago that they should climb the stairs to explore the top chambers, and to get a better look at the area around them. The Captain agreed, and the two of them began the ascent.

"In truth, Captain Santiago, I had a strong desire to climb the pyramid at Coba. I had planned to do that as the men explored that city. But the old man convinced me that we should leave, and I didn't get the chance. I believe that we shall be able to see for miles up there, and I can't wait to get to the top."

"I felt the same way, Captain. Leaving Coba without climbing to the top of that temple was a huge disappointment for me, also. Have you noticed how narrow these steps are? The Mayans must not have been very big people."

"I suspect you're right. The Indians we have with us are not big men, either. They say that these Mayans are their ancestors, so your theory does make sense."

"But looking at the incredibly huge structures that they built makes you think that they were an industrious people, not afraid of a challenge."

"Certainly not, Captain, these Mayans were truly an amazing people!"

They took the last few steps to the terrace that surrounded the chamber room. The view was spectacular, and didn't disappoint them. They could see every building in this city from up there, and they even thought that they could see the Caribbean off in the far eastern horizon. They circled the terrace, and took in the view in every direction. The Yucatan spread out below them in a forest of green.

Captain Montero was the first to break the silence. "I can't believe how beautiful it is from up here. I can see the Coba pyramid, Nohoc Mul, from here. Do you see it?"

"Yes sir. It is an unbelievable sight to behold. But did you notice that there seems to be no housing here, like we saw in Coba? Most of the buildings here seem to be temples or ceremonial sites; I wonder where the people of this city lived?"

"This city must have served a different purpose for the Mayans. The Chief did refer to this as a sacred city. Perhaps only their Holy Men lived inside the city; maybe the people lived in the surrounding area."

"That is a very valid theory, Captain. But I see no sign of any Sacred Well, do you?"

"No, you're right. I don't see anything like that either. But there is a sacbes leading east of the temple that goes into the woods over there. Do you see it?"

"Yes, now I do. Do you suppose that's the way to the Well?"

"It must be. It's exactly where the old chief said it would be; east of the Temple of Kukulcan. Let's see what's inside here, before we descend."

The two men entered the chamber through a stone entryway in the center. There was a solid stone wall in the center, but there was room on either side to go around. They each went a different route, but ended up in the same place. They were standing at the back side of the temple stairs. They went back into the chamber. The light was dim in there, but the men couldn't help notice that the walls were stained red. They both realized at the same time that this must have been where the ritual sacrifices were performed; the walls hadn't been painted, they were soaked in the blood of humans who had given their lives to the Serpent God.

Neither Captain wanted to spend much more time here in this chamber of death. They both moved to the front entrance, and immediately began the long climb down. There was no idle chatter this time, only the sounds of their feet tapping on the stone steps. The ground came up fast, and both men collected themselves as they stepped down and onto the packed earth.

As they walked away from the Temple, Captain Montero realized that they both had acted a little too fearful. But the chamber was an evil place, and he certainly had no desire to climb those stairs again. "Thank God that they had taken the time to view the scenery before they entered Hell," he thought.

"Well, Captain Santiago, I trust that you too saw enough of that place? I think we should get the men together to discuss our plans for today."

"Yes, Captain, that's an excellent idea! And yes, I have no interest in going back into that room. One can only wonder at the torture and gruesome deaths that took place there. I plan to stay on the ground in the future! I will call the men together now, sir."

CHAPTER 15

Chichen Itza, That Same Day

"**M**EN, we have observed the city from the top of this temple, and have not seen anything unusual. But before we begin our exploration at the Sacred Well, we want to be sure that we are the only ones here. Break up into groups of three, and start going building to building throughout the entire city. Don't miss anything; we want no surprises here today. Make sure that there is no one else to stop us from completing the task ahead. Captain Santiago and I will stay here with the Indians and establish a base of operations. Report anything unusual to your sergeant, and don't do anything foolish."

The men did as they were told. They began to spread out in different directions around the city. Each temple and building was searched, but nothing was found.

Like Coba, there were many buildings in the trees that had been overrun by vines and bushes. Large trees grew up through some of them, but the buildings that were in the open near the big temple seemed to be clear. It was as if someone was still using them; they might have just left yesterday. But the men doubted that was the case.

Perhaps the old Chief was right; no Indians would come near this place.

All you had to do was look at the Indians from Coba that accompanied them here. Fear was in their eyes; it was only a matter of time before they'd disappear again, leaving the Spaniards without help. But for now, they unloaded the provisions and set up the camp for the soldiers. Who could tell if they'd be here tomorrow?

As the men reported back to the camp, they began to settle in for the night. Captain Montero had told them to stay together in a large building that opened on to some kind of playing field. The Captains had taken up residence in some chambers above the rest of them. They all wondered what kind of game was played here, for it resembled nothing they had ever seen before.

After eating, some of the men relaxed and talked about what was ahead of them the next day. Nobody knew for sure what this Sacred Well was, but they would know soon enough. Captain Montero had made it very clear that he intended to start the search for treasure tomorrow. They drifted off, one by one, to go to sleep, or to stay on watch. They needed to be ready; tomorrow was sure to be an exciting day!

CHAPTER 16

Sebastian, Florida
July 16, 1996

THE seas had finally calmed down after the tropical storm that had ripped up the beaches a few days before. The water had laid down, and the sands along the coast had settled back into the nooks and crannies of the sea bottom below. Visibility was at about 100 feet underwater, and on the East Coast of Florida, that's about as good as it gets. The gin-clear water and calm seas meant only one thing around here; it was time to go treasure hunting.

Fortune Salvors was one of the outfits that showed up every summer in Sebastian, along with a handful of other hunters. They docked at the commercial docks, and many of the divers stayed in local hotels near the river. It wasn't exactly a tourist boom, but any extra money in the summer was a good thing, so everybody always made them feel welcome. Most of the divers thought of themselves as 'swashbuckling adventurers', and when they weren't looking for treasure they were usually spending most of their money in the bars and taverns along the water. The local merchants loved them, as long as they weren't tearing up their place.

This was Sue Morgan's third season in Sebastian. She had joined up with Fortune Salvors two years before, after finishing up her second tour of duty with the Coast Guard, and she was one of the few employees who had made the choice to call Sebastian home. She had rented a small house on the river, close to the docks where her company kept their boat when they were diving. It was a small square-shaped, stucco house with a flat roof that leaked whenever it rained hard, but the view she had was worth the trouble. Her landlord had been promising to fix the old flat roof soon, but it had been fourteen months since she moved in, and the roof still leaked. Maybe he'd get to it, she always told everybody; the truth was she wouldn't trade her little place for anything. She absolutely loved living on the water.

It was still dark as their boat made its way out of the channel, heading for the Sebastian Inlet. The Indian River was very shallow in most places, and it had protected manatee zones everywhere, so going slow was the only way to get out to the deep water. The ride out in the morning was one of her most favorite times, though, so the slower, the better. A glint of the coming sunrise could be seen off in the distance, but the moon was still lighting up the sky behind them. It was forecast to be a perfect day for diving; no wind, no storms and plenty of heat, but she'd be in the water most of the time, so that wouldn't be a problem.

The team had been working a new discovery just north of the Inlet before the storm came in. They had brought up mostly artifacts so far, but a large pile of ballast rocks that had been found made them feel that they might be close to something bigger. Ballast rocks were thought to be a roadmap for treasure hunters; usually a ship went down with its ballast in the bottom of the ship. Over time, much of the boat's timber would rot away, leaving a pile of rocks. Finding a pile of ballast was seen as a strong omen that the ship's cargo would be nearby, buried under sand and coral. It was their job to find the booty and bring it to the boat. The spot where they had found the rocks was on the boat's GPS, so they knew that they'd get another chance today.

Diving with underwater metal detectors, the team would cover a particular grid around the site. When they completely scoured the grid they were working, they'd move into the next and repeat the process. The boat was equipped with a unique device that aided the divers as they were searching. There was a large tube that was fitted over the props from both of the big outboard engines; the *propwash* tube attached to a large flexible hose that the hunters would use to blow away the sand and debris around the area where they got a metal reading. Treasure hunters affectionately called this device a 'mailbox', probably because it delivered the goods! If there was something under the sand, using the mailbox would usually expose the item. It was tediously slow work, but the rewards could be worth a year's pay, so each day Sue and the other divers went about their work, taking turns down below, waiting for the big find.

In the days after the storm Sue and some of her crewmates spent some of their idle time drinking beer and shooting the shit at Earl's Hideaway. Earl's was one of those places where the locals hung out, but nobody there cared where the treasure boaters were from because they all had good stories to tell. They swapped treasure hunting stories with some of the local fishermen, who dazzled them with their stories of huge fish at the Inlet, or hundred pound tarpon up in the North Fork of the Sebastian River.

Last night they had wrapped up their evening pretty early after only having a couple of drafts. The boat would be pulling out at 5 am, and if they weren't on it, their boss would fire them for being stupid. Sue told the boys that she had a really good feeling about tomorrow; she thought that it was going to be a great dive, and that they'd find something really cool. Everybody drank to that and went their separate ways.

Now they were moving through the Inlet, and the sun was starting to break the horizon in front of them. Once they were in open water, she saw that the weatherman had been right; the seas were flat and there wasn't a cloud in the sky. Looking into the water below her, she saw fish of all sizes scattering beneath the decks of their boat. It was going to be a special day!

CHAPTER 17

Chichen Itza
February 24th, 1714

CAPTAIN Montero called the men together in the morning. He explained their mission once more to them; he wanted to be sure that his men would perform their task, and be loyal to him, but more importantly, to King Felipe'. He told them how critical it was to Spain's future that they do their job and get the treasure back to the King. When he sensed that the men were all in agreement with his pronouncements, he told them it was time to go to the Sacred Well. The real adventure they had talked about for days was about to start.

Captain Montero and Captain Santiago led the way down the eastern sacbes. It seemed to be moving downhill at a slight angle, and there were cuts in the soil beside the road that must have been washed out during heavy rains. But the road itself was remarkably solid, and offered no problems for the men.

They walked for about a half mile, when they saw a large clearing up ahead of them. They quickened their pace, and entered into the clearing. At the far side of the clearing they could see a solid wall of stone, not man made, but natural. It resembled a stone quarry; the walls were grayish white, and more than likely were limestone, which seemed to be everywhere in the Yucatan.

The wall dropped into a glistening pool of water. They knew that this must be the Sacred Well; there was a stone altar at the edge of the cliff nearest them, perched on a large flat stone. The well seemed to be a cenote, like others they had encountered. Captain Montero walked out on the stone, and stood near the altar. Looking down into the pool, he saw that there was no apparent way to get to the water below. The cliff face around the entire well was a sheer drop, at least one hundred feet to the water below. The water stared back at him, a silent pool of green that seemed to be daring him to find its mysteries.

"Captain Santiago! We're going to need lots of rope. There doesn't seem to be any way down these cliffs, except to rappel down. There is a ledge just above the water line on the far side of the pool that we can use as a staging area. Find out who our best swimmers are, and get them down there as soon as you can. I want to find out how difficult our task is going to be, and whether or not there is treasure in these waters."

Yes sir! Sergeant! Have the men tie some lengths of rope together, and send your best men down there to that ledge. They can begin to explore the water as soon as the gear is down there."

"Yes, Captain! But I think that we'll need more rope for this work than we have with us. Perhaps I can go back to camp, and have our Indians make us some more. Baskets would be a good idea, also. We can pull them up once they are filled."

"Excellent, sergeant. Dispatch the men, and go back to camp. Get back as quickly as you can."

"Yes sir!"

The remaining men worked their way over to the far side of the cenote. The brush and vines here were thick, and almost impenetrable. The path along the cliff was precariously close to the edge, so they had to be very careful with their footing. No man wished to join the spirits of this place.

As the men got to the clearing above the ledge, Captain Montero yelled out to them. "I'll give an extra bonus to the man who brings me the first piece of treasure from this place. Hurry my friends, and you will be rewarded."

The men were lowering the rope down to the ledge. When they heard the Captain's offer, they suddenly all wanted to be the first man down the rope. The Captain's words had worked their magic; the men were now fighting over who went over the cliff. It was decided that their remaining sergeant, Sergeant Ramirez, would be the lucky man.

The sergeant made his way to the edge of the cliff. The men had tied the rope around each other, and they were ready to begin the descent. Grabbing the rope firmly, Sergeant Ramirez went over the side. His feet touched nothing as he snaked his way down to the ledge. Minutes passed, and the sergeant was about twenty feet above the rocks when he called out that there wasn't enough rope; it was too short.

"Pull me back up! We'll have to wait for more rope to come from camp."

The men began to haul the sergeant up. He was nearly at the edge, when one of the men in front had the dirt under his feet begin to crumble. They all slipped, trying to hold on. Sergeant Ramirez bounced hard on the rock face, and lost his grip. He fell the hundred feet to the rocks below, crushing his skull. His body slid off the ledge, and was swallowed up by the dark green water.

The Captains, watching from the altar stone, were the only witnesses to the sergeant's death. The others only heard his screams and the cold crack of bone as he hit the rocks.

CHAPTER 18

Chichen Itza, That Same Day

Aﬀter the accident at the cenote, the Captain decided it would be a good idea to go back to camp. He knew better what they needed to complete their task, and decided to take some to time to prepare for their next assault on the Well. He thought that they could retrieve the body of the sergeant once they got into the water. He ordered the men on the far side of the cliff to take everything and return to the sporting field.

His mind was racing as he walked back along the sacbes with Captain Santiago. He shouldn't have pushed the men so hard; they should have been better prepared to descend the cliff to the water below. He was sure that the men thought him responsible for Sergeant Ramirez' death, but there was nothing more he could do other than make sure that this type of tragedy didn't happen again.

"Captain Santiago, I feel very badly about the sergeant's death. It could have been avoided if we had taken the time to get the proper gear in order. We must go back and put everything that we need together before attempting to go back into the Well. In addition to ropes and baskets, I think that we should make some sort of float-ing platform that we can lower into the water. The men can use the platform to dive from and to collect whatever they might find."

"That's an excellent idea sir. We could attach ropes to it to pull it across the pool. I was thinking that we should have the Indians construct a rope ladder that the men could use to get in and out of the Well. It would be much safer for them."

"Yes, and we must find a way to anchor it, since we found out that the topsoil around the cliff is not very sol-id."

"Perhaps we could tie it to the stone altar. I don't think anything will move that. It must weigh a thousand pounds."

"You're probably right, Captain. I don't think we'll find a more secure spot, since there are no large trees anywhere near the cliff sides. Have the men work on building our work platform, and have the Indians contin-ue making their ropes. Have them construct the ladder, as well."

"I will do that, sir. Is there anything else, Captain?"

"I'm going to my quarters right now. I'll continue to think on what else we need, and I'd like you to ask the men if they have any ideas that we might consider. Please let me know if there's anything that makes sense; we need to be sure of success this next time."

"Yes sir! You're right about not wanting to meet with failure again; the men must know that we are ready to do the job that we came here to do."

With that, Captain Santiago left to join the men. He

gathered them together and offered a prayer for Sergeant Ramirez. Ramirez had been with him since the beginning, and the Captain knew that he had lost one of his best men. But he also knew that he needed to name a new sergeant from amongst the remaining men, and he thought that since everyone had been together for some time, it now made sense to let one of Captain Montero's marines take a leadership position.

"Lopez, I am promoting you to Sergeant effective immediately. I want you to take a group of men into the forest to cut down enough trees to build a floating work platform that we'll use at the well. Take one of the Indians with you to identify the ones that will float the best."

"Yes sir, thank you, sir! I am honored to be your sergeant, Captain. I will take some men there now."

"Good, Sergeant. Sergeant Sanchez, I want you to take some men and cut hardwood rungs for a rope ladder that the Indians will build. Make sure that the wood is strong, and bring at least one hundred or more. We must get this started as soon as possible. Have some of your men go with the Indians to gather what they'll need for making the ropes. They will need to make many lengths of rope to construct the ladder and the platform. Once they have enough to get started, have all of the Indians working on the ropes; your men can go back into the forest to continue the gathering. Keep working on these assignments until dark, and we'll get started on them again in the morning."

CHAPTER 19

Sebastian, Florida
October 2nd, 2004

It hadn't taken Ray and CJ long to get back on their feet. The drunks always seemed to walk away from the wreck, right? Bumps and bruises, with a few minor cuts, were the worst of it for the boys.

They were sitting at their new *favorite place*, Fisherman's Landing. Despite the nice name, the bar was about a half step up from the old Scales & Bones, but it seemed to them that the women here were easier. Hell, they were heroes to most of the locals, having ridden out the big storm sleeping under the bar. There was no shortage of people who wanted to buy them a beer, and they enjoyed every minute of their time there.

But they were getting bored. They hadn't gone this long without taking their boat out to the Inlet to fish. They needed to check their crab pots, too, if they could find them. Nobody was going out on the river because of the wrecks and tree debris everywhere, and the Coast Guard was still telling people to stay onshore. But this was interfering with how they made money for beer and weed, so staying in any longer wasn't part of their plan.

After knocking down one last beer before leaving, they decided to haul their old boat out of Ray's pole barn in the morning, and get out on the water. CJ said he'd call when he got up, and Ray thought that was a great idea. He knew CJ would never be up at the crack of dawn, so he'd get to sleep in a little bit, too.

They climbed into Ray's old Ford pickup. In a moment of complete sobriety, they had renamed the truck *Jeanne* in honor of the storm, since it was the only thing left standing after their night at the pub (unless you counted Uncle Bob's cypress bar, but who the hell named a bar anything!). They left the parking lot real slowly; Sebastian cops were known to sit around Indian River Drive, just hiding and waiting for innocent folks like them.

They went up Davis St. to U.S. 1 and took a right. Trying not to attract attention, Ray kept the truck in the right lane, making sure he wasn't going over the speed limit. He'd done this so many times over the years that it seemed like Jeanne could do it by herself. He'd only been arrested once, and lost his license for three months that time, but his buddy CJ had lost his license for a year the last time they got him.

He took a left on Roseland Road, and just past the tracks he took a right down to Bay St. He was doing good. He dropped CJ off at his mother's place, and took off for Vero Lake Estates out by the Interstate. Ray had inherited his old man's place after he had died five years ago of cancer, and him and CJ called it the *Shack*, but it really wasn't bad. As they say, the price was right, and it came with a fairly new pole barn out back.

He didn't have much of anything, so when he got the

house, he just left everything where it was and moved his clothes in. He put the old boat in the barn, and promptly got drunk, thanking his old man for everything. Life had seemed to work out quite well for Ray Eldridge.

behind. She also told me that Savannah was the *'Irish Capital of the South'*, and that it would be just like being home It wasn't.

CHAPTER 20

Boston Police Headquarters
April 17th, 1977

M E and my crew had been thrown into a holding cell with all sorts of lowlifes. We sat there for over six hours before two detectives came in. One of them called out my name, and the other was looking for Paul Callahan. They led us to separate interview rooms; I was with a big guy who looked kind of familiar. The big cop sat me down hard in the chair, and handcuffed me to the table. He lit a cigarette, and slowly walked around the table.

"So you know you're in some serious shit, don't you son?"

"I didn't do anything wrong."

"Oh my Lord, can you believe it? I've arrested another innocent Irish boy from Southie! I don't know why we even have a station down there, with all you saintly kids running around."

"That's pretty funny, Officer."

"It's Detective, Mr. Smart Ass! Or, I should say, Mr. Burke, shouldn't I? Big John's boy Jackie; I bet the old man is real proud of you these days; a real chip off the old potato, eh?"

"I haven't talked to my father in months. I wouldn't know."

"Oh, you mean since you beat the shit out of him when he came home so drunk he could barely stand up? You got some balls, kid, I'll tell you. I heard John would like a rematch, but your mother told him if he laid another hand on you she'd leave him, and take the kids away. I heard he's more worried about the problems she might cause than kicking your ass, so I guess you're safe, for now."

"I wouldn't know, Detective."

"You know what else you don't know, Jackie boy? Your friend Tim died in the bus on the way to Mass General, and so did the driver of the vehicle you guys were trying to *jack*. That's a whole lot of shit coming down on your little gang, mister. But you want to hear the worst part, son?"

"How could it get much worse than that?"

"Oh, it's much worse. The driver was somebody you know quite well; she was the mother of an old school friend of yours. Does the name *Catherine Buckley* mean anything to you, Jackie?"

My mind flew to scenes from years past; I had spent so much time in this woman's home with my friend Seamus. I had been there on weekends, holidays, watching Red Sox games, all kinds of things. She was one of the nicest people that I had ever known, and her husband, Mike, was a great guy, too. He was a Boston fireman who rarely ever drank anything more than a beer or two, and he treated his wife and kids like you could only dream about. The Buckley house had been a *safe haven* for me many times when Big John was on the rampage, and I couldn't remember a mean word ever being spoken in that house; it was pure *Ozzie & Harriet.*

"Are you saying that Mrs. Buckley was the driver? And she's dead?"

"As dead as your buddy Tim."

"Oh, shit! I can't believe it; what the hell was she doing with a gun? Why didn't she just give up her damned car?"

"You tell me why she fought back. Don't you think she was as scared as she ever was in her life when your boy Tim came at her with a crow bar? And she probably had a gun because she was worried about punks like you and your crew threatening her. Jesus Christ, Jackie! What a dumbass you are! What the hell ever happened to you? You used to be a good kid!"

"How do you know so much about me? Who are you?"

"Does the name *Dougherty* mean anything to you? As in, the Dougherty's who live down the block from where you grew up? As in *Bobby Dougherty*, the kid you and Seamus used to come to the park to watch play baseball?"

"No way! You're Bobby Dougherty? I thought you got drafted and went down South to play baseball. What are you doing back in Boston?"

"I did play in the Orioles system for two years, but during the winter before my third Spring Training I took a girl from Florida out to a ski resort in western North Carolina. She had never seen snow in her life, and

I thought it would be a kick to take her out there. She had taught me quite a bit about surfing, so I thought I'd return the favor and teach her to ski. She caught on to it pretty quickly, and on the fourth day we were there, we decided to try a tougher course. As we were going down the mountain, I was trying to keep an eye on her, and keep her close. Since I was paying more attention to her than where I was going, my ski caught a submerged branch, and I went flying ass over teakettle. I hit a large tree, and my leg was shattered in about fifteen places. The local doctors did their best, but I never played baseball again. That's when I came home, went to Mass Bay Community College, got my degree in Law Enforcement and joined the force."

Detective Dougherty and I talked for over an hour about baseball, the Red Sox in particular, and other local events. Eventually the detective stood up and changed the subject; he really wanted to get as much information as he could about my social group. He quickly went from being one of the old neighborhood boys to being a cop again. Personally, I liked him a lot better when he was one of the kids from the block.

"Look, Jackie, enough about old times. I want you to tell me whatever you can about your activities over the past few months. I need some help solving some cases we think you and your boys were involved in. You're not even eighteen yet; I can help you if you co-operate. Tell me some good stuff, and I'll make sure that you get probation, and not jail time. Walpole State Prison is not a fun place to be for a boy your age, Jackie, I promise you. It doesn't matter how tough you are, that place will destroy you; it's the worst shithole prison in the Northeast!"

I thought about this for a minute. Bobby Dougherty was right about the prison thing; I had no desire to spend any time there, because I knew that quite a few of Big John's boys lived there, and I wasn't too sure that any of them would offer me a friendly hand once I was inside. Bobby Dougherty was throwing me a lifeline, and I sure as hell was gonna grab it!

I told my story to the detective; he already knew that it was Tim Hogan who had shot the driver, so the rest came easy. I told him about some of the burglaries he was interested in, and even gave him the name of my Puerto Rican friend in Dorchester. Without giving it all up, I managed to satisfy the cop enough to get an agreement.

"Well, Jackie, you're doing the right thing. I'll make sure that your deal goes through with the D.A., and I'll walk it by the Judge. But you're going to need to get the hell out of Boston, because there's going to be some pissed off Irish gentlemen who won't be happy with your talking, or your walking."

"Oh, and Jackie, just so you know; it was one of your old man's boys that tipped us off to your job last night. We picked him up two days ago for all sorts of things, and he sang like a bird about you and your boys. It seems his nephew is one of your crew; after some hard drinking at Leary's a few nights ago, your man told his uncle about everything you boys have been doing. He even gave him your favorite spots for the carjackings, and told him you guys were pulling one in the next few nights, so we've been sitting on all of them for the last couple of nights. When he told us about your crew, he added that the info was courtesy of Big John. Your Da wants to see you locked up, Jackie, and that's definitely not a good thing for you!"

I was released from the jail later that day. I called my Ma and asked her to meet me for breakfast the next morning at O'Toole's, a neighborhood diner near my old house. When we had settled in and ordered, I told her everything, and promised her that I was ready to start over, but I needed some help. Detective Dougherty had told me to get out of Boston, but I had no idea at all where I could possibly go.

She told me that we had some family in Savannah, Georgia, one of her cousins. She called her cousin and made arrangements for me to rent a room with her, and I left on the Greyhound bus the next morning. My Ma promised me that she wouldn't tell anyone, especially Big John, where I was. She told me that I should change my name and leave Boston.

CHAPTER 21

Chichen Itza
February 27th, 1712

SEVERAL days had passed as the men worked to build what they would need. The raft, or platform, was done and ready to launch. Some of the men had carried it down to the cliff nearest the stone altar, and it sat there as the men finished everything else that needed to be done.

The Indians had built a very strong ladder that was at least a hundred feet long. It had been tied to a side wall of one of the stone temples, and had been tested. It, too, was ready. Everything seemed to be in place, and the men made their way to the Well once more, carrying the rest of their equipment with them. They were ready to begin again.

Captain Montero gathered his men. He knew that many of them still blamed him for the accident four days earlier, so he wanted to assure them that their safety was a concern for him. He told them all to be careful, and to work in pairs, so that no one might get lost in the waters of the well.

Two of the men tied the ladder to the base of the

stone altar. They took great care to make sure that their knots were strong, and when they finished checking, they sent the ladder over the cliff. The bottom of the ladder splashed into the water below, and the men cheered.

Captain Montero had decided that it would be best if several men went down into the water to be ready to secure the raft as it was dropped into the pool. Sergeant Lopez' men were chosen for this assignment, since being marines, they were naturally the strongest swimmers of the group.

One by one, the men descended the ladder. When the four men chosen were in the water, the Captain ordered the platform to be dropped. It dropped very quickly and made a huge splash. The four men swam to it, and climbed on. A long rope was thrown down from the top, and it was tied to a post that the men had built into the front of the raft. From the other side of the cliffs one of the men threw a second rope down to the float, and it was secured to a post at the rear of the platform. With the two ropes anchoring the raft, they now had a working platform that they could not only move around, but one that could be drawn back to the ladder whenever their time in the water was done.

They could begin the search! Captain Montero planned to only have eight men in the water at one time. They would work in four groups of two, and then be replaced by another eight swimmers as they rested. Each group would work for an hour. He felt that would be the best way to maximize the search capabilities of his men.

Four more men went down the ladder to join the others. Tying ropes to themselves, they tied the other end to the raft. Each of the men took a deep breath and dove into the water. The Captains and the rest of the men watched the water as air bubbles surfaced from below.

Heads began popping up out of the water. The swimmers yelled up that they couldn't find a bottom to this well, and that they needed to go deeper on their next dives. One of the men, who had done quite a bit of sponge diving as a boy in Spain, suggested that they hold a large rock to their chest as they jumped back in, so that they could go deeper before running out of air.

Captain Santiago had the men lower some limestone rocks down to the men in the raft. Each of them picked one, and holding it to their chest as their friend had suggested, they all dove back into the water. Again, the men up top waited for some sign of success.

Two groups rose to the surface, then three. They all wondered where the last two men were. Suddenly they saw a bright shiny object rise out of the water. The sponge diver had something! It was a large knife, with an ornate handle that looked like silver. The blade was made of sharpened obsidian, a stone so dense that it could be sharpened like glass. Cheers went up amongst the men.

"Did you find the knife on the bottom?" asked Captain Santiago.

"No sir. I don't think there is a bottom to this pool. I found it on a large rock ledge. There are more things there; I need to go back again to see what else is there."

"The rest of you look for large rocks or ledges below the water then. That may be our only hope of treasure" said Captain Santiago. The eight men once again picked up rocks and dove in. They had moved the raft over to where the sponge diver had found his knife, and all of them were concentrating on that area. All but two of them landed on top of the ledge; the others released their rocks and swam over. Each of them fanned out quickly, and began to find items on the rock. They grabbed what they could and pulled themselves up with their ropes.

Five of the eight surfaced with something that appeared to be valuable. The others had what appeared to be wooden urns. They put their finds on the raft, and held them up for the others to see.

There was some sort of helmet or headdress that was covered in silver and gold. The sight of the gold in the helmet brought more cheers from the men; this was going to be a treasure hunt after all.

Each of the divers held up their prize. There were two more knives, both inlaid with gold and silver. There were three tablets, or plates, that had raised heads of the gods like the men had seen carved into the stone temples throughout the city. These appeared to be silver.

The remaining three men that had found the sealed urns put them into the basket to be raised up to the Captain. Everyone at the top wondered what was in the wooden vessels; what could it be that seemed to be so special that the Indians had cast them into the pool along with the treasures they sought?

Captain Montero handed one of the urns to Sergeant Sanchez, who was standing nearby. The urns were sealed with something sticky, so the sergeant took out his knife and cut into the seal on the jar. Turning it upside down, he emptied it on the stone altar. What happened next shocked all of the men.

Dozens of small gold and silver pieces spilled out of the urn and sparkled in the sunlight. There was also jewelry of gold and silver, and trinkets of lesser metals.

In the middle of the pile sat something that seemed to be reddish, but it was hard to identify. It was very dried up; perhaps it might have been food or something else for the Gods. Then one of the men saw that the gold and silver pieces and jewelry seemed to have a reddish cast to them, as well.

It was then that Captain Montero realized what it was that they didn't recognize. "I believe that what we have here in this urn is the remains of a human heart. The Indians must have used this vessel to contain their sacrifice. These urns are more valuable than they would appear."

With that, the remaining two urns were opened by the sergeant. As the Captain had anticipated, these too were full of treasure, and of the remains of the sacrificed. The divers were now very excited about getting back in to the water. New divers entered the water every hour, as they had established. They dove again and again, until it was dark.

Many of the dives were unsuccessful, but the Sacred Well continued to give up its treasure.

CHAPTER 22

Harbor Branch Oceanographic Institute, Fort Pierce, Florida, May 13th, 1988

PETE Harris stood listening as the marine biologist told the assembled group about the work that he and his team were doing there at the Institute. The professor was working on several projects that dealt with raising shrimp and crawfish in large plastic tubs they jokingly called *'fishbowls'*. Their work was being done in greenhouse-type structures on the back side of the campus; the real trick was that they were actually making progress on what could eventually change the way the World eats seafood.

If the group continued getting the strong results that were showing up now, a whole new branch of aquaculture would be born here. Aquaculture farmers anywhere in the world would be able to follow the same procedures being developed here, and add millions of pounds of shrimp and crawfish annually to the diminishing harvest of the oceans and backwaters everywhere. This breakthrough, the Professor stated, was like Eli Whitney's invention of the Cotton Gin, something that changed the garment and textile industry and brought it screeching into the modern era. The shrimp tubs could be placed anywhere; they didn't need to be near a saltwater source, since the water they used was fresh, and the infrastructure could be built in a jungle or in the city. It was a pretty amazing feat, Pete thought as the Professor's words sank in.

Pete was working on his Doctorate in Marine Archeology, but had spent the last two summers here at Harbor Branch working on some of the various projects going on at the campus. Anybody who got to help out on these projects was considered to be very fortunate; the men and women running the programs here were very selective as to whom they hired, even on temporary assignments. Pete's former Marine Biology professor had called some old friends at the Institute and had given him a strong recommendation, because Pete was into anything cool going on with the ocean and The Indian River Lagoon, two of his favorite places. It didn't hurt that his minor throughout college was Marine Biology; he still thought that he could end up in that field when the dust cleared, so why not spend some quality summer time here changing the world?

He was older than most of the other students there. He had spent some time in the US Coast Guard years before, and had ended up stationed right here in Fort Pierce, on the Seaway. After he got out, he decided to stay in the area, and went to college on Uncle Sam. He graduated with a degree in History, and then worked on getting his Master's Degree in Marine Archeology. It was the old 'Atlantis theory' that had drawn him in; it had to be out there somewhere, right? So he decided to spend some time looking for that and anything else below the water; it seemed like a natural fit for a guy like him who lived to dive and loved history. It was his dream combo!

When Pete wasn't studying, diving or fishing, he spent a lot of time with his favorite guitar. He couldn't remember when he started playing, only that his mother had taught him early on how to strum that Gibson. She claimed to have been Arlo Guthrie's girlfriend at one time, and claimed to be with him on that fateful *'Thanksgiving Day Massacree'* at Alice's Restaurant, back in Massachusetts. He didn't know about all that, but she sure taught him to love music. He never did develop a great singing voice, but he figured that if guys like Arlo, Dylan and Jimmy Buffet could make it big, then he'd concentrate on playing the same kind of tunes; throaty, raspy, folksy stuff.

To supplement his student income, Pete had taken a regular job at Archie's, over on A1A, on the beach. Archie's had been there for so many years it was almost a beachside institution itself. Bikers, locals, tourists, or whatever; everybody came to the place to have some fun. Pete played his guitar and sang his songs three nights a week, and tonight was a work night. He needed to get going; enough shrimp for today!

CHAPTER 23

Chichen Itza
March 1st, 1714

THE men had been diving continually for three days, and it seemed that they had found everything that they might discover in the Sacred Well. It would be dark in a few hours, and Captain Montero was ready to pack up what they had found and get ready for the journey back to Tulum. As he was pondering whether to call the men in, one of the men on the raft called up to him. It was the sponge diver, Ramon de Silva, whose ingenuity had brought them their treasures.

"Captain, I have another idea. Would you like to hear it?"

"Of course, Ramon, what is it?"

"It would seem to me that directly below the altar is where we might have found something valuable, but we found no ledge there. Since we have covered every inch of this pool, perhaps I could try one last time to see if there might be something down deeper in that spot. I'll have to use a larger stone, but I'm sure that I can do it."

"Then please, Ramon, go ahead with your plan, but

be careful."

A large rock was lowered down to the raft in one of the baskets. It was twice the size of the stones that they had been using, and Ramon had trouble lifting it. When he raised it to his chest, he took a deep breath and jumped into the water. His rope went tight, and then it loosened up a bit. The men waited as his air bubbles appeared around them.

After almost three minutes, Ramon's head and shoulders burst through the surface. He held up something that sent a chill through every man; it was a headdress of solid gold! They hadn't recovered anything like this in the three days of searching; this was truly the greatest prize yet!

The men were still cheering as Ramon cried out "Captain, I saw something else down there. It, too, seemed to be golden. I must go back one more time!"

"Then rest for a moment, Ramon, and dive again! Certainly, it would seem to be worth the effort."

After a few minutes of rest, Ramon repeated his dive preparations. When he was ready, he plunged into the green waters again. The three men on the raft with him peered over the side, looking for a sign of Ramon and his new find. Every man on the cliff above watched and waited, just as anxious as the men below. And then they saw Ramon's head rising from the water. The item he now held was the most remarkable thing that any of the men had ever seen.

It was a golden chain, with thick, heavy links. The chain was about six feet long, and the links seemed to get smaller as they got closer to one end. At the thickest end there was a cast golden form; it was a serpent's head with fiery red eyes. The chain was actually a six foot long golden snake!

The *Golden Snake* took the men's breath away. It was a spectacular find! Ramon had been right; this was the richest location yet. Could there be even more still?

Ramon had handed the 'snake' up to one of the other men on the raft. The man had put it into one of their baskets, and it was pulled up to the altar for everyone to see. As Ramon clung to the side of the raft, trying to get his breath back, he felt a very vicious bite on his leg. Pain raced through his body, as he began to lose consciousness. As the men above him cheered and danced, Ramon de Silva sank back into the water. He was dead before his head went under, and his body descended and settled on the ledge where he had found his prizes.

Nobody had been watching Ramon, and nobody had witnessed his death. Their eyes had been on the Golden Serpent and nothing else. Nobody saw the large snake that slid up onto the raft until one of the other men screamed out in horror! He, too, was attacked and bitten, and fell to the edge of the raft and into the water as quickly as Ramon had gone before him.

The other two men frantically ran to the rope ladder. As they fought to get off the raft, the big snake swung around and came after the man in the rear. It struck him with a savage bite before the man could get to the ladder. He would not live to see the next minute, and he, too, fell into the darkening water below him.

The men on the top of the cliff, frozen to inaction by what they were seeing below them, hadn't moved quickly enough, but they started to pull the rope ladder up out of the water. They pulled the man up as fast as they could, but it wasn't fast enough. With a final lunge, the great snake caught the last diver, and tore into the man's foot. His screams could be heard everywhere, but it was too late. The serpent held on and dragged him below the water, where he joined his companions in the deadly depths of the Sacred Well.

CHAPTER 24

Sebastian, Florida
October 3rd, 2004

THE next morning Ray got the call from CJ. It was 9:30, about the time he had expected to hear from his buddy. He had just gotten up a half hour before, and was working on his second cup of black coffee. He picked up the phone.

"Hey Sunshine, you finally get your sorry ass out of the sack? I been waitin' on ya for hours now."

"Bullshit, Ray! You ain't been up for hours; I probably just woke your ass up callin' ya!"

"Yeah, Yeah, right! You wish, asshole! You ready to git goin', or what?"

"No, I need to help my old lady with somethin', I don't know what. All she's doin' is bustin' my ass since I got up."

"Well, you go help your Mommy, boy, and I'll get the boat ready. Call me back when we can go do some fishin' and drinkin'. Don't be wastin' any more of my time!"

"Yeah, like your time's so damned precious! You wouldn't know what to do with yourself if I didn't keep you busy. I'll call ya in a while, man. See ya!"

An hour went by; Ray had gotten the boat out of the barn, and loaded up their fishing gear. CJ kept all of his stuff here, because he was afraid his mother might sell it off at the pawn shop on U.S. 1 to get some of the *rent* money he owed her. Like she had a chance of making any money from his junk, but he couldn't risk that she might try.

He hooked up the boat to Jeanne, and took the truck and boat down to the gas station on CR 510. He filled up both tanks, since the truck was already on fumes from their adventures the last few days, and grabbed two twelve packs of Natural Light from the cooler. It was God-awful beer, but it was cheap, and the guy who owned the place kept a good stock of it there for him and CJ. What the hell, he mused. "It got you drunk; wasn't that was beer supposed to do?"

His cell phone began to play *Freebird*. He loved that damned song, so why not have it as his ringtone, right? He looked down at it. It was CJ. "Hey man! You ready, or what?"

"Yeah, I'm ready. Pick me up out in front of Wal-Mart; that's what I had to do with the Old Lady, but we're done. How long ya gonna be?"

I'll be there in ten minutes. I got the boat gassed up, and picked up some beer. Get some ice at Wal-Mart while you're waitin. See ya soon!"

"OK, buddy! I'll be here. Man do I need a beer, too. My head's killin' me."

It's killin' me , too! Oh shit, I meant your face; your face is killin' me!"

"Up yours, Ray! Get your ass here; I'll go get some ice."

CHAPTER 25

USCG Station, Pensacola, Florida
February 12th, 1976

LIEUTENANT Rick Perry had made it out of Vietnam, and had initially found himself stationed in Jacksonville, Florida for a short time before being reassigned to the base in Pensacola. The western Florida Panhandle city was home to one of the largest Naval Air Stations in the country, and Rick had gotten used to the sounds of jets and turbos overhead after a few weeks. The NAS was home to the Navy's Blue Angels, and he got to watch them practicing their maneuvers almost every day. His heart quickened, though, at the sound of the big helicopters that passed over his station regularly, and he remembered how much flying helos had interested him back in 'Nam.

Things were a lot safer here back in the States; a pilot didn't have to concern himself with RPG's and machine gun fire, so Rick's mind kept wandering back to the idea of becoming a search and rescue helicopter pilot. He found out that there was a big training center just across the bay in Alabama that trained Coast Guard officers to become pilots, so he had finally applied for the program about a month ago. He had just received a call from the Station Commander to come to his office; he was on his way.

"Good morning, sir. You wanted to see me, sir?"

"Yes, Lieutenant, come in and sit down. It's about your request for Helicopter Training, Rick. Congratulations, you're going to Flight School!"

"That's fantastic news, sir. I've wanted to fly choppers since I was stationed in Phu Quoc, in Vietnam. I thought that the timing was better now than ever before; this is exciting!"

"I thought you'd like the news. You're enrolled in the next training group starting in two weeks; you'll have to go through Initial Flight Training, then you'll be moved up into active helo training when that's done. Your training will be in Mobile at the USCG Aviation Training Center; it's a great facility, and the commanding officer is an old Academy buddy of mine. I gave you a very strong recommendation when his staff called about you; I'm expecting big things from you, Lieutenant."

"Yes sir, thank you, sir. Does it say when I should report for duty?"

"It does. You need to be there on the 24th for registration and assignment, and your training will begin two days later. Why don't you get your gear packed and take a few days off before heading over there? You'll be working seven days a week for long hours every day, so a little R &R won't hurt before you get started."

"Thank you very much, Commander. I really appreciate your endorsement, and the time off. It's been a pleasure working under you here in Pensacola. Will that be all, sir?"

"Yes, Rick. Enjoy your training, and *Semper Paratus!*"

"Aye, sir. *Semper Paratus!* Thanks again, Commander!"

CHAPTER 26

Chichen Itza, after the tragedy

CAPTAIN Montero and Captain Santiago had seen the attacks on their men. They stood, like all of the other men, around the top of the cliff, shocked at what had happened below them. As the water settled down, and became still once more, the *Golden Snake* in the basket had almost been forgotten. It was on the stone altar in front of Captain Montero.

"Men, I cannot tell you how saddened I am by what just happened to those men. The cruel way in which they all died is something I will never forget, and I'm sure none of you will either. Let us pray to God that these men will find peace with the Father in Heaven, and that their families will not be punished by the Fates in the years ahead. May God rest their souls."

The men assembled at the altar with Captain Montero and prayed for several minutes. When they were finished, the Captain said "I think the time has come to leave this evil place. We will take what we have now, and leave for Tulum in the morning. Let's go back to camp and prepare for our departure then."

He took the basket with the Golden Snake, and Captain Santiago carried the golden headdress. The soldiers carried the rest of what they had found, and they all made their way up the sacbes towards camp.

When they got back to their camp, the Indians were nowhere in sight. It seemed that they had taken their belongings and had left. A search party was sent out to find them, but came back with no news; the Spaniards were alone once more.

The Indians had heard the blood-curdling screams of the last victim of the serpent. It struck fear into their hearts. Every one of them had grown up hearing the legends of their ancestors, and this place was the holiest of all of the Mayan cities. It was said that the Serpent God, Kukulcan, lived here, and protected his people from everything imaginable. The soldier's dying screams were enough to convince them that they should leave this place immediately, and no Spaniard was going to keep them here for anything more.

The soldiers packed their gear, and readied for the morning march. They ate a meal, and settled in for the night. Tomorrow would be the first day of a very tiring march back to the sea.

They left Chichen Itza on the morning of March 2nd, 1714. The week that it took them to reach Tulum went by without any unusual incidents. Expecting problems with the local Indians on the way back, Captain Montero had been sending out scouts each day in advance of their party. The scouts had encountered no problems, however, and the trip ended up being rather uneventful.

They entered Tulum and set up their camp as they

had when they were there the last time. The Captains decided that since they were on familiar ground, one or more of their men might decide to take some of the treasure for themselves and desert the camp. They chose four of their most loyal soldiers, and together with them, they set up a watch on Captain Montero's chambers. The Captain's quarters seemed to be the most defensible position, so they had put the treasure in there.

Before departing Tulum, they had made arrangements with Lieutenant Del Castilla to bring the Nuestra Senora de la Ascension back to the city twice a month, and to send a longboat into the camp to see if the Captains had returned. They didn't know that the ship had been taken by British Privateers just three days after departing Tulum. There would be no longboat from the pirated ship, but they wouldn't know that for weeks to come.

CHAPTER 27

Tulum
May 15th, 1714

CAPTAIN Santiago and Captain Montero sat sipping tea. They had been in Tulum for five weeks, and there had been no sign of the Nuestra Senora de la Ascension. It was decided between them that Captain Santiago would take four men with him, and go to the garrison at Coz-Mel. Once they arrived there, the Commandant would send a ship with men and supplies to rescue them.

Captain Santiago gathered his men, and they prepared for the trip up the coast. He would leave immediately. The heat of summer was upon this place, and he knew that it would be an arduous journey. He thought that it would take him four or more days if they followed the roads along the shore, so it was important to get started. He didn't like the idea of leaving Captain Montero and his few men with the treasure, but they had decided that this was best.

On May 27th, Captain Montero heard a cry from one of his lookouts on the cliff. The man was saying that he saw a ship approaching from the north, and that it would be here soon. Two hours later, Captain Santiago stepped off one of the longboats, and greeted the Captain.

"Hello, again Captain Montero! I'm glad to see that everything seems to be alright here. How have you been?"

"I've been fine, Captain! You are truly a welcome sight! Please come ashore and tell me of your trip."

Captain Santiago related the story of their journey to the Spanish fort. He told the Captain that they had not seen any of the local Indians along the way, which he found to be rather strange. They had been told that many of the Indians lived along the shore, fishing and farming the nearby land, but they had not seen a single one in the four days that it had taken them to get to the beach opposite Coz-Mel. It had seemed to him that these modern day Indians had disappeared like their Mayan ancestors before them.

"When we got to the beach across from the garrison, we built a large bonfire. Within a few hours, a boat arrived from Coz-Mel to find our encampment. When we told them who we were, they loaded us up and took us across the bay to the town. I met with the Commandant immediately, and told him of our plight. He had already been ordered by the Admiral to assist us if we needed his help, so he ordered the captain of this ship to prepare to sail for Tulum at first light. And here we are!"

"Excellent, Captain! The rest of the men and I are ready to leave this place; let's get the men working on loading our equipment and supplies first, and then we'll load the treasure last, as a safety concern."

Captain Santiago had brought ten men with him from the ship. The new men introduced themselves to the veterans, and everybody began to pack up their belongings. The longboats were filled, and went back to the ship. One boat returned to get the Captains and the treasure. It was filled with armed marines, as Captain Montero had ordered.

The soldiers loaded the treasure baskets into the longboat. These men had not been with them on the trip to Chichen Itza, so when they saw some of the artifacts, they were stunned by their beauty. Not believing what they were seeing in the baskets, they continued to load the boat as they had been told.

When the last basket was on the boat, the two Captains looked up at the cliffs and temples of Tulum. Though neither man spoke, they were both thinking that they were glad to be leaving this land that had cost them so many lives. They entered the longboat, and never looked back.

The trip back to the garrison from Tulum had been pretty uneventful. Calm seas, and strong breezes, had gotten them to the island in no time. On the second morning after arriving in Coz-Mel, the captains both arose to a great hub-bub from the central square of the fort. Men were bustling about, carrying and pushing all sorts of barrels and crates, and all of the activity seemed to be heading towards the docks.

Captain Santiago arrived in the plaza just before Captain Montero. They both marveled at the activity, not really sure what was happening.

"Captain, it certainly seems that there is something important going on here this morning. I wonder what the reason might be?"

Captain Montero shrugged his shoulders, and yelled out to one of the men going by. "Soldier, what is all the excitement about?"

"The Governor received orders from the Admiral in Havana from King Felipe', who has ordered all ships from Nova Espana and Cartagena to meet in Havana, and depart as soon as possible. The four ships from Vera Cruz that have been waiting for your arrival from Tulum are already provisioned, and ready to depart. We must leave today, to join the Armada from Havana to Spain."

"Then I think that we should meet with the Commandant and the other ships captains to go over our plans. We must hurry; it seems that we're the last ones to join the party!"

CHAPTER 28

Sebastian, Florida
October 3rd, 2004

Ray and CJ were working on their third *'Natty'* when their boat hit a sandbar just west of the State Park on the south side of Sebastian Inlet. The bar had never been there before, and the surprise of being up in the mud almost sent both of them into the water.

"Sheeee-it! Where the hell did that come from? We're in the channel, ain't we?"

CJ, who was busy trying to figure out what had just happened, answered that he thought they were, but it sure didn't look that way. Their boat was littered with fishing gear, their lunch, and the entire contents of their cooler. Cans of beer rolled around the boat, and their sandwiches were now soggy from water that had been in the cooler; it wasn't looking like such a good day anymore.

"I don't understand why we're up on this muck", Ray said. "I've run through here a million times, and never had no problem!"

"Well, the Coasties been saying that everything's different in the river than it was before the storms. That damned Jeanne must have changed the bottom out here. That's the only thing that makes any sense."

"Yeah, you're probably right. I damned near lost another tooth on my beer can, for God's sake! Well, you gonna get out and push us off, or what?"

"Why me? I ain't the horse's ass who run up on the bar; you should take that honor, asshole!"

"I suppose you're right; if I don't do it, we'll never get fishing."

As Ray got in the water to push the boat off, he saw that there was a new cut south of the park, between the old Treasure Museum and the South Gate, and it looked like ocean water was coming into the flats. He remembered hearing somebody at the bar saying something about A1A being shut down, so this might be why. "Hey, CJ, check it out; it looks like Jeanne cut a new inlet through Ambersand Beach. I'll betcha there's some fish coming through that!"

"Holy shit, you're right! I didn't see that comin' out, but it would make sense that there's some fish feedin' over there. Let's go see what we got!"

As the boat slid off the sandbar, Ray jumped back in the boat and started steering towards the cut. He was real careful to go slow, watching the bottom as he drove through the sea grass. There was a bunch of pompano skipping around out in front of them, apparently enjoying their new found playground. They stopped the boat, and set up their rods with pompano rigs, using sand fleas for bait. They both tossed their baits into the pompano, and it wasn't long before they were pulling in some nice fish.

"Hell, we'll have a cooler full of these babies pretty soon, Ray. We can certainly sell some of them for beer money; I'm sure people will be *Jonesin'* for some fresh fish back in town."

"Oh yeah, these little darlins will definitely bring us some pocket change, for sure! Let's sit on these fish 'til they stop bitin.'"

The two men tossed in fresh baits, and cracked some new beers. They'd lost most of their ice, and what they managed to save was being used to keep the fish cold, so the beer was getting a little warm. Neither one cared, though; they were fishin' again, and drinking beer, and who gives two shits anyhow if the beer's warm?

An east wind had started to blow in from the beach, cooling them off a little bit. They hadn't noticed that the breeze was also pushing the boat, causing their lines to tighten up. Finally seeing that his line might be snagged, CJ got up and gave a tug on his pole. It grabbed the bottom, and wouldn't come off.

"Son of a bitch! I'm stuck on something back there; I can't get my line free."

"Jesus, now we're gonna scare off every friggin' fish in that spot. What a dumb shit thing to do, CJ!"

"Man, I didn't mean to do that. I was just enjoying the day, and lost track of my line; wind tightened us up, is all."

"Yeah, yeah, I know; blah, blah, blah! I'll bring the boat up slow, and you keep trying to get loose."

Ray brought the boat in closer to the spot, but CJ couldn't release his line. As they got closer to the snag, CJ saw something shiny on the bottom, right around where he was caught up. It seemed to be large, whatever it was, and the reflection in the water grew bigger as they approached it.

"Hey, Ray, hold up; there's something shiny as hell on the bottom, and I think it's what I'm stuck on. I'm going over the side to check it out."

They were in a spot about four feet deep, and CJ went below the surface for a minute. As Ray waited for him to re-emerge, he laughed to himself that his old buddy was warm beer drunk, and was gonna come up with some real *trophy* for sure! The water in front of him started to boil up, then CJ's head popped up. He brought up something that looked like a big gold chain, crusted with all kinds of shit. As he was about to get back into the boat, he screamed out in what Ray later described as 'a banshee howl', and disappeared into the water again. Ray ran to the front of the boat, looking into the water, but couldn't see a thing. Whatever was going on was obscured by the mud that had been stirred up. Afraid to go in himself, he waited to see what would happen next.

Minutes ticked off, and the water began to settle. Even though he had his fishin' glasses on, he couldn't see a thing moving around him; he slowly began to move the boat around in a small circle, continuing that for about ten minutes. On his third loop, he saw CJ's body on the bottom, thirty feet from where he'd gone in. Fearing whatever had gotten CJ, Ray grabbed his long handled gaff, and reached into the water. He hooked CJ's jeans, and pulled him up as fast as he could.

He got CJ's feet over the side, and grabbed him with all his strength. Pulling him onto the deck, Ray turned him over onto his back. He recoiled in horror as he saw what had killed his friend. There was a hole in his chest the size of a volleyball, and CJ's heart had been ripped out of the middle of it!

Barely able to contain himself, Ray gunned the engine, and got out of there as fast as he could. He headed for the boat ramp back in Sebastian, with tears streaming from his eyes. His best friend ever lay dead in his boat, and he was as scared as he'd ever been in his entire life! He managed to get out his cell phone, and dialed 911. He told the operator at the station that she needed to get somebody down to the North Boat Ramp on Main St. just as soon as she could. When she asked what had happened, he could only reply that he had no idea.

CHAPTER 29

Havana, Cuba
June 1st, 1715

THE five ships had arrived in Havana just before dark. Unable to do much else, they had anchored in the harbor, and several longboats carried the officers and some of the men into the port city. Because of the vast amounts of treasure that the ships had on board, at least fifty marines guarded each of the ships at all times. The Privateers weren't a problem here inside the harbor, but this amount of gold and jewels could entice any man to steal his own fortune. The most important treasures were placed in the Captain's quarters, since it was deemed that it was the safest place on any ship, and it was guarded heavily by the most loyal soldiers. The marines were ordered to kill anyone who came near the treasures, and they would carry out their orders without hesitation.

The next evening, the officers of the five ships were brought to the Governor's Palace, where they were greeted by both the Governor and the Admiral. There were dozens of other officers of various ranks in attendance, all in their finest uniforms. It was quite a splendid affair, not unlike the court of the King himself, with servants running everywhere to make sure that the officers were well taken care of. Beautiful women dressed in elaborate gowns filtered through the crowds, showing off dazzling jewelry, no doubt cast from the plundered lands of Nova Espana. The oppressive heat and loss of lives seemed to be a distant memory for everyone that had spent time in the Yucatan or the other regions of the territory.

The Admiral had introduced the officers to the commanders of the two Spanish fleets. Captain-General Don Juan Esteban de Ubilla, was the commander of the *Flota de Nova Espana*, from Vera Cruz. His ship, the *Capitana*, would have the richest treasure of any of the ships. The *Esquadron de Terra Firma*, the southern fleet, was under the command of Captain-General Don Antonio de Escheverez y Zubiza. The *Terra Firma* fleet consisted of six ships, and served the trade routes out of Cartagena, to the south.

The two fleets had been in the New World for almost two years, putting together one of the richest treasure cargoes ever assembled. From Vera Cruz, they had gathered over 3 million silver coins, many chests of gold coins, gold and silver bars, and jewelry. From the Manila galleons coming from the Far East, they had gotten pearls, emeralds and Chinese porcelain. The *Esquadron de Terra Firma*, from Cartagena, had also brought many chests full of gold and silver coins, gold bars, gold dust, jewelry, and precious tropical spices. Now, under direct orders from King Felipe', they were to prepare their ships for the trip back to Spain.

The Admiral named Captain Don Diego Montero as

the commander of the *Nuestra Senora de la Concepcion*, with Captain Don Pablo de Santiago in charge of the soldiers and marines on board. The two captains had been received very well in Havana, due to their adventures in the Mayan cities and the incredible treasures that they had brought with them. The Mayan cache would remain with them on their ship, and they would also be given a large amount of gold and silver coins to carry back to the King.

As the evening wore on, the officers of the fleet enjoyed their time at the Governor's Palace. No one suspected that it would be another seven weeks before their fleet would sail from Havana.

CHAPTER 30

Savannah, Georgia
November 15th, 1977

I GOT a job in a local supermarket, bagging groceries and helping to stock the shelves. It was the most boring shit I'd ever done, but it was honest money, and I was keeping out of trouble. I had changed my last name to *Buckley*, in honor of Mrs. Buckley, and went by *Don*. To all of my new acquaintances in Savannah, I was just *Don Buckley*, supermarket geek. It worked for a few months.

In addition to changing my name, I decided to get my High School GED. When I took the deal with Detective Dougherty, I had really taken a hard look at myself and the life that I'd fallen into. I now knew that I wanted to do better than that, so I enrolled in a local program and passed the test with flying colors.

After moving to Savannah, I'd struck up a friendship with a girl who worked with me; her name was Charlotte Wilson, and she was a true *Southern girl*. I was crazy about the way she talked, and the way she flirted with me without being slutty. The big city girls back home in Southie were always throwing themselves at me; Charlotte wasn't like that. I couldn't wait to see her whenever I went to work; I think I remember having difficulty breathing or talking a few times in her presence, so I'm pretty sure I was falling in love for the first time. If the crew back home could have heard me then, they'd surely have thought I'd lost my mind.

A couple of months had gone by before I decided to ask her out on a date. We talked about it, and Charlotte hit me with a couple things I hadn't planned on.

"You know, Don, that Momma was telling me that you're probably one of those Irish Catholics. My family doesn't take kindly to Catholics, so that's a problem for me. I don't want to get involved with a boy who's not going to college, either. My man is going to have to be somebody that can support his wife and family, so going to college and getting a good job is important to me."

"God, Charlotte, I just wanted to go to the movies, or dinner, or something. I didn't just propose to you. And I wouldn't consider myself a Catholic; it's true that I'm Irish, but I stopped going to their church years ago. College isn't out of the question, either, you know? I'm looking at entering the Community College downtown for the second semester. The counselor I met with there said that if I worked hard, I could probably get through the required courses in a year and a half, if I went to Summer School, too. Then I could apply for entrance to a university somewhere to get my degree. That's what I'm planning to do; I start classes on January 14th."

"Well, Don, that sounds much better, but before we start dating, why don't you come to my church with me and my family on Sunday? I know they'd all like that, and we always go for a nice brunch down on River St. after; what do you say, Don? Are you in or out?"

Before I knew what I was doing, my lips started moving. I told Charlotte that it would be fine, and that I'd be looking forward to it. The deal was done; I was going to church.

CHAPTER 31

Savannah, Georgia
November 18th, 1977

I WAS standing outside of a beautiful old church; it was a Methodist church, and it was quite old. Like so many other buildings in Savannah, just like Boston, the church looked like it was probably built a long time ago. There was an old graveyard beside it, and the entire property was immaculately landscaped. I was waiting for Charlotte and her family to show up; I couldn't believe that I'd agreed to this, but once I did, I knew I had to do it. I wasn't sure what to expect, and I had no idea what a "Methodist" church even was, but I think that I would have done anything to be anywhere with my Miss Charlotte.

Charlotte and her family came up behind me. "Good morning, Don", she said, and smiled at me like she never had before. "This is my Father, Tom, my Mother, Joan, and my two brothers, Christian and Joshua. Have you been waiting long?"

"Uh, no, not long at all. Nice to meet you all, I'm Don Buckley, but you probably all know that already."

"Yes, we do, Don", her dad said. "We're glad to have you with us this morning. Charlotte has told us a lot about you. We better get inside; we're running a little late."

We entered the old church, and I was struck by the fact that it didn't look like any Catholic church I'd ever been in. The architecture was very simple, unlike St. Mary's back home. The pews weren't in rows, but were boxed in like small cubicles. Missing were the big statues and stained glass; it was actually quite spartan. There was a large cross hanging on the back wall, and a raised pulpit, like the one at St. Mary's, but these were the only similarities to the Catholic Church I had attended in South Boston. Mr. Wilson led the family to a box close to the pulpit; I thought that the family must be somewhat important here to have their own space so close to the pulpit.

"Was somebody saving these for you?" I whispered, as we filed in to our seats.

"No, silly, this has been my family's box for almost two hundred years; they were founding members of this church when it was built in 1785, and were given this pew box as a reward for their generous contributions to the building fund. Most of my ancestors were buried outside in the cemetery until the 1950's; they ran out of space, and there was no land left around here to buy. I imagine that we'll always have our pew box, though."

The minister (as Charlotte had called him) had walked in, and he made his way up to the pulpit. He raised his hands, smiled, and welcomed everyone to the service. After saying good morning to him, the congregation settled in, and waited for him to begin the Welcoming Prayer. He led the people through the Lord's Prayer, and paused for a moment. Looking out over the assembly, he began talking about a homeless man that he had seen downtown the day before. He went on talking about the man, and how this man was one of God's flock, just like the rest of us. As I listened, the minister's words touched me; I began to feel that what the minister was doing was a very good thing. He was making everyone understand that in God's eyes we were all equal, and that everyone deserved to be treated well. As he went on with his homily, I found myself riveted by his impassioned speech.

I, Don Buckley, aka Jackie Burke, realized for the first time in my young life that there might be something bigger than me; it was an epiphany for me, one that would change my life forever. I enjoyed my time at the church, and it became a ritual that I looked forward to for several weeks more. And then 'Life' came roaring back on me!

CHAPTER 32

Sebastian, Florida
October 8th, 2004

"Y'ALL take care, Ray. Real sorry to hear about CJ; he was a good boy."

"Thank you Mrs. Allen. We really appreciate you and your family comin' out here today to pay your respects." Ray and CJ had gone through twelve years of school with Mrs. Adam's son Clayton. Clayt had played football and baseball with the boys for years, and they had been good friends. Clayt had joined the Marines after they graduated, and had said that he wanted to retire a Marine just like his granddaddy had.

His grandfather had spent time in the Pacific Theater during World War II, and had gotten a Purple Heart and a Silver Star. He had signed on again after the war, and ended up spending twenty years in, including two tours in Korea in the early 1950's. Wounded again while rescuing several men in his platoon, he received a second Purple Heart and a Distinguished Service Commendation for his efforts. He had climbed to the position of Gunnery Sergeant in a Marines Weapons Platoon before retiring to Sebastian just before all hell broke loose in Indochina. He was called back up as a reservist for two years just after the Tet Offensive in Vietnam in 1968, but never left Florida.

Clayt had grown up idolizing the old soldier; his grandfather loved to fish and hunt, and he had taught Clayt everything he knew about both. He talked about the Corps, and how proud he was to be part of the best fighting machine in history. Clayt was hooked, and couldn't wait to sign up and get to Parris Island, South Carolina, for his boot training. He loved the daily grind that every Marine went through, and he became a *hardcore jarhead* in no time.

On February 21st, 1991, just a week before the conflict ended, Lance Corporal Clayton Allen became one of the 148 casualties of the 1st Persian Gulf War, known more commonly as *Operation Desert Storm*. Clayt was with his squad when they were attacked by insurgents just outside of Tikrit, Iraq, and was killed instantly when a mortar round hit his Humvee.

Clayt had been sent home with full military honors, and Ray and CJ had been pallbearers at his funeral. He was buried in the city cemetery on Route 1, and hearing the twenty-one gun salute and the sound of *Taps* being played as Clayt was lowered into the ground had been the toughest day in Ray's life before today.

Ray said thanks to everybody else one by one. He and CJ's mother were the only family that CJ had, and they both were amazed by how many local folks had come out to the old Fellsmere Cemetery out on County Road 512. Everybody in CJ's family had been buried there, thanks to his great-grandfather buying a family plot, but it was outside of town, and they really hadn't expected too many people to drive out there on a hot day like today. But CJ's bizarre death had been the only thing anybody was talking about around town, so it was probably just morbid curiosity that brought many of them out.

The official report said that CJ had been killed by a shark that had come into the river following the fish, or by a bull gator, out of its normal element. Those seemed to be the only explanations for what had happened to CJ Hilton, but Ray was the only one who thought differently. He would have seen something if it was either of the two; big sharks and big gators don't just disappear like they'd never been there before. But what the hell was it that tore his friend's life from his chest?

Ray hadn't been sleeping too well since the day of the accident. Every time that his eyes closed, he saw the vision of his best buddy being dragged under by something evil; not a shark or a gator, but something straight from Hell. Nights now were for fear and cold sweats; he stumbled through each day like he was dead himself, not knowing what to do or say. And now his friend was gone forever; the worms would start eating him before the end of the day, and they'd never go fishin' again. "What would he do with the rest of his sorry-ass life?"

CHAPTER 33

Havana, Cuba
July 27th, 1715

WEEKS had passed since the fleet had made their preparations for departure, but the embarkation day had finally arrived, and the eleven ships of the Armada were leaving the harbor en route to Spain. Storms and privateers had kept them inside, but the Navy had done its job, sinking or capturing every pirate ship in the immediate area, and the seas had calmed. King Felipe' was anxiously awaiting the treasure that the ships held, so the decision had been made by the Admiral to leave at once.

Once again, as was the custom, the officers of the ships had been feted by the Governor on the eve of their sailing. A grand event was held, and everyone agreed that it was time to get on the open sea. The time everyone had spent sitting around Havana had been tiresome, and there wasn't a man amongst them that didn't want to feel a fresh ocean breeze on his face. The Governor and Admiral wished them well, and they prayed together to the Virgin that they would have a safe trip.

As the morning breezes began to fill the sails, each of

the ships made their way out of the harbor, staying close to each other for protection. Even though the Navy had assured them of the removal of any pirates, the amount of treasure on these ships was enough to bring men from far away to claim a share. They needed to be watchful at all times.

The Admiral had assigned four *Men-o-War* to the fleet for added protection. Each of these big warships carried fifty to sixty guns, and had as many as two hundred soldiers on board. They would escort the fleet across the Straits of Florida to safer waters along the Florida coast. They would return to Havana once the Captain-Generals felt that they were no longer needed. Another group of warships from St. Augustine, the Spanish stronghold in Florida, would be waiting for them further north, and would escort them out to sea. After that, the ships would be on their own until they reached Spain. Even after the wars, Spain still maintained control of the major shipping routes from the New World to Europe, and their ships were everywhere along these lanes, so the Admiral felt that he had done everything he could to ensure their safe journey home to Spain.

In addition, every ship in the fleet carried an extra fifty soldiers each, and these ships carried thirty to forty guns also. The Admiral and his Captains wanted to take no chance of being overwhelmed by any privateers that they might find waiting for them, because their King needed every ounce of treasure on every ship. Not delivering it to him would be unacceptable.

During their seven week layover in Havana, several freakish deaths had occurred. They were all fairly violent, but two of them had been gruesome. All of the deaths had happened on just one of their ships, the *Nuestra Senora de la Concepcion*, Captain Don Diego Montero's ship. The sailors, and even some of the officers, had begun to call it the *Death Ship*, since it was seemingly an ill-fated vessel. Every man who had been killed was a marine assigned to guard the Captain's quarters, where most of the recovered treasure from New Spain was being kept, and each of them had been savagely bitten by something. Two of the victims had their hearts ripped from their chests; nobody had ever seen anything quite so horrific.

CHAPTER 34

South of Sebastian Inlet
July 16, 1996

THE captain pulled up on the big boat's motors and settled over a spot that wasn't more than forty feet deep. The anchor was thrown over, and after it grabbed on the bottom, he shut the motors down. Two of the guys grabbed the big prop cover, the 'mailbox', and started attaching it to the mounts on the stern of the boat; when they had that secured they screwed the big hose onto it and dropped it over the side. They let everyone know that it was *showtime*, and immediately went to put their gear on.

There was six divers total on the boat, including the captain. They worked in pairs, a tank at a time, while the others either rested, or hopefully worked on any recovered treasure that they might have brought up. There was always something to do, so the day passed quickly, shift-to-shift.

Sue and her partner, another former Coastie, had the second dive. Eric Trombley, a local guy, was quite a legend around town; he was a three sport letterman in high school, and was quite a ladies' man. What Sue really liked about him, though, was the fact that when he went in the water, he was dead serious about getting the job done. They had started diving together last year after Eric's old partner moved out to Texas to work on an off-shore oil platform, and Sue had taken a real shine to him. She was like an older sister to him, and they did everything together when he wasn't chasing younger women on shore. Lots of people in town speculated that she and Eric had something going, but she had her own story; she had left her heart with someone else, and hadn't ever gotten it back. She hoped that he still knew it was his.

The first team came up after a while, and dumped some bags on the dive platform. They were smiling, so everybody figured that they must have found something. Eric and Sue were ready to go in, but they lingered while the wet team opened their bags. There was some ceramic stuff, a rusted pistol and a chunk of coral that glistened in the sun. Gold coins were frozen in the coral, and there were lots of them! They told Sue and Eric where they had found them, and told them that they had left a marker down there along with the hose.

"What are you two waiting for? Jesus, get your sorry asses in the water, and go find us some more of this sparkly rock. You were right last night, Sue. Today is going to be a special day!"

"Gotcha! We're going in. See you soon!"

They swam towards the marker that the first team had left; they could see it clearly from following the hose. When they got to the spot, they pulled on the hose to let the guys up top know to start the engines again. They started searching the grid with their metal detectors and immediately got pings from both. Eric started working the mailbox over the area, washing the sand and silt away from the metal that was lighting them up.

As he moved the hose back and forth over the spot, Sue caught her first glimpse of something very shiny. With a small pick that she carried, she pulled at the sand and coral below her, exposing a clump of golden coins encrusted with coral. It was almost identical to the one that the guys had brought up just a few minutes ago. She bagged it, and gave Eric a thumbs up. He was already over a second spot where he had gotten a strong reading. The hose was working its magic, and soon he, too, had a clump of gold coins.

Sue had kept her detector working while she helped Eric with his find, when the machine started pinging again just to her left. Eric bagged his gold, and moved the hose over to her. They both spotted another chunk of coral loaded with golden coins and pried it loose. Not wanting to miss anything they both went back to work; their tank would be gone soon, and they were on a streak like no other.

As she slid sideways to a new spot, she was suddenly stricken with a very sharp pain in her left side. It was excruciating; she had to get up to the boat fast, but wasn't sure that she could even make it. She motioned to Eric that she needed to get out of the water, but he thought she was crazy. They still had air left; what could she be thinking?

She knew that she had to get to the boat; the pain was becoming worse. She kept waving to Eric, and started swimming to the surface. He reluctantly started to follow her, but she never saw him swim up behind her. She passed out, and drifted off into a dark place.

CHAPTER 35

Sebastian River Medical Center
July 18, 1996

SUE opened her eyes slowly; she felt like she'd been run over by the north-bound Florida East Coast Railway! She couldn't figure out where she was at first, but she soon realized that she was in a hospital room somewhere. She had smelled the antiseptic odor first, and then glanced around the room. "How did I get here," she wondered?

As her eyes moved around the room, she saw a familiar face sitting in the chair next to her bed. It was Eric, and he looked like shit!

"Hey dude, what are you doing here? You look like you been on a bender for a couple of days!"

"That's funny, girl, 'cause I been thinkin' you don't look so hot, either!"

"Nice! What the hell happened to me, Eric, and where am I?"

"Do you remember when you signaled me to go up early, before our tanks were done? You started swimming back to the boat, and I reluctantly followed. I didn't know what was going on, but I could sense that something wasn't right. As you swam towards the boat, you suddenly stopped short and clutched your chest; you started sinking. I grabbed onto you and swam you up to the platform; the guys pulled you onboard. The Captain called in a *'Mayday'* on the radio, and the Coast Guard answered the call. They told us to get you to the beach as fast as we could; they had one of their birds in the air just over Vero Beach, and they said they'd be there in two minutes. We got the boat in as close as we could, and Tom and I got you onto the beach in the dinghy. The Coasties were there landing as we hit the sand; they loaded you up on a stretcher and brought you here. You're at Sebastian River."

"Oh my God! I can't believe it. All I remember after we started finding the gold coins was having a killer chest pain. Everything else is gone."

"Well, you were almost gone, girl. Your doctor will be in soon, but I can tell you that you're a very lucky lady. They said you almost died; they're still not sure how you made it through."

The harsh reality flooded over her as she started to get her bearings. She did remember trying to get back to the boat; she was almost there, but…what? She didn't have a clue what had happened after she blacked out, but two days had gone by, and she was here in a hospital room very much alive.

"What about the treasure? Did you guys keep bringing it up?"

"The guys went out yesterday and today. Without a partner, I couldn't dive, so I've been hanging out here waiting for you to come around. They're absolutely killing it out there, though. The coins keep coming up on the detectors; yesterday Tom found a big ass pile of silver coins. They must have brought up hundreds, according to their stories. They all came by last night to see you, but you were still out cold. They went out again today, but they'll be by tonight, for sure."

"That's incredible news! Is the boss happy, or what?"

"Oh, he's happy as a clam! The guys were telling me last night that he hasn't stopped smiling since the first bag of gold coins came up the first day; except when he's worrying about you, of course."

"Yeah, right! I'm surprised he hasn't gotten rid of me yet; he hasn't had a good year for quite a while, so I wouldn't be surprised to find out he's replacing me soon."

"Unfortunately, you won't be able to continue your diving career, Miss Morgan, so your boss will have to re-place you. Your condition won't allow you to work in any kind of strenuous position; I'd suggest a good desk job. My name is Dr. John Mackin; I'm in charge of your care while you're here."

Neither one of them had seen the doctor come into the room. They had been absorbed in the details of the treasure hunt, and Sue was just getting used to being awake and alive again. His abrupt news left both of them in a state of shock; her, more than Eric.

"Doctor, what are you talking about? What is my condition?"

"I'm afraid that what you went through in the water was just a sampling of what you might be in for in the future if you don't curtail your active lifestyle. I was seri-ous when I said a desk job would be a good idea; at least something that won't put a strain on your heart. What you have Miss Morgan, is an abnormality in your heart; your aorta, to be more precise. It's not a rare condition, but we don't see it very often. As you get older, the problem increases, and can very often be deadly if not caught soon enough. You'll need to make changes from now on to ensure that you're taking better care of your heart. We'll talk about a diet plan, and what you're able to do as far as exercise goes in a couple of days. For now, just rest up and get on your feet."

"Well, okay, I guess. You've managed to knock me for a loop, Doc. I spent seven years in the Coast Guard on two different tours, and I've been diving and swimming my entire life. It's a big part of the reason I settled here in Sebastian two years ago; this is where my life is now, on the water. Are you saying that I'll never be able to do those things again?"

"I'm afraid I am; it's too dangerous to play with. You can find plenty of other things to do on the water around here; buy a boat, learn to fish, or go to the beach. Just keep away from the swimming and diving, okay?"

"Okay, okay. I suppose that having my own boat to tool around with isn't such a bad idea. I'll spend some of my treasure share on one; fishing's actually something I enjoy."

"Just keep to fishing for trout and redfish; no big tarpon or offshore fish. Light duty only."

"I should probably thank both of you for keeping me alive, by the way. Really, guys, thanks!"

The two men smiled, and the doctor left the room. Eric told Sue that he was going home for a nap and a shower, but he'd see her later, when he'd return with the rest of the team. Giving her a light peck on the cheek, he backed out of the room, still smiling as he closed the door.

CHAPTER 36

Off the Coast of Florida
July 31st, 1715

JUST after daybreak, the ships began to get tossed about by huge waves that had come up during the night. Driving rain and howling wind beat against the ships, and it seemed that the decision to leave Havana last week was not such a good one. The storm was fierce, and began to shred the sails of every boat; masts cracked, and everything on deck flew about, being thrown around as if weightless. As the storm became more intense, the ships lost sight of each other. Waves twenty to thirty feet high were smashing against the sides, and over the rails, lifting the boats wherever they wanted to. The Captains of every ship did whatever they could to keep their ship afloat, but one by one they drifted in towards the shore, into shallow water, where they struck reefs that ripped holes in their bellies, and sent their treasures spilling into the sands below. Seven hundred men lost their lives that day, as the Ocean reclaimed the treasure that man had taken from its sister Earth.

The *Nuestra Senora de la Concepcion*, one of the larger galleons in the fleet, was luckier than most for a while. Its captain, Don Diego Montero, was a highly skilled sailor, and had managed to keep his ship under control longer than most. But when the waves that crashed over the ship were thirty foot high, he couldn't maintain control, and like most of the others before him, his ship crashed on the reef, and sank to its death. None of the men from *the Death Ship* ever made it to shore like some of the others, so nobody ever knew where the ship had gone down. The survivors thought that it was good that the ship had disappeared, taking its evil with it. Many of them blamed 'the Death Ship' for what had happened, and prayed to Jesus and the Virgin for helping them survive the worst day that they had ever seen in their lives.

CHAPTER 37

The Florida Coast
August 6th, 1715

HUNDREDS of survivors had managed to swim or float their way to the beaches along the coast, but only one of the survivors was a Captain on one of the ships that had gone down. The Captain, Don Pedro Jesus de Avila, had stayed with his ship until the end, and had somehow ended up on the beach alive. He had no recollection of when he actually went into the ocean; he could only see the massive walls of water that had been slamming his ship, crushing it beneath their wake. Whenever sleep came to him, he was caught up in violent dreams of the huge waves taking him and his men to the bottom, only to wake up to find himself very much alive and in charge of the remaining sailors and soldiers from the fleet. He thanked the Virgin for her help in his rescue, for certainly there was some sort of *Divine Intervention*.

Captain de Avila had come ashore in an area that was near a natural inlet that appeared to be a river mouth. He had gathered the other survivors in the area together and had set up a campsite for the salvage work that needed to be done. The camp was to the north of where many of the ships had gone down, but the wrecks closest to this area seemed to be in relatively shallow water, and would be the easiest targets for his men to reclaim their precious cargoes.

He sent men in both directions for miles to gather any other survivors. They were told to come to the camp he had set up to prepare for the retrieval efforts. All of the Spaniards that had made it to the beaches made their way to the camp, and joined the other survivors in establishing a working salvage location. Dozens of other men were sent out to bring back anything that could be used in the camp; lumber, ropes, sails, rigging, clothes and weaponry were the most sought after, and the men were very successful in finding these things along the beach.

The men had found two longboats that were still serviceable along the beach, and were able to find some oars that hadn't been destroyed. The Captain ordered six men to take one of the boats across the inland waters to the river's source; they needed fresh water to get through the intense heat of each day here. He sent another eight men out; four to the north and four to the south, on exactly the same mission. They were instructed to find fresh water springs and food sources. He knew that without food and water, his men would all die here on this desolate strip of land, so finding both was more important than going after the treasure at this point.

On their first trip up into the river, the men in the longboat had discovered that they were not alone there; as they had rowed along the banks of the river they had seen Indians on several occasions. The Indians didn't seem to be hostile; they would just stare at the Spaniards as they went by. The men continued their search until they were rewarded by finding a very large freshwater spring close to the river; the water was clean, unlike that of the river, which still had a salty flavor. Saltwater could be a sailor's worst enemy, so finding the spring was critical to their group's survival. The Captain would be pleased, they thought.

They had brought several large barrels with them that had washed up on the beaches. As they filled these with the fresh water and loaded up the boat, they noticed that a small group of Indians were watching them from the nearby trees. They knew that this would become a regular job for them each day, unless the men that were dispatched to find a water source along the beach were successful, so they made an attempt to speak to the Indians and show them that they were peaceful in their intentions.

Several of the male Indians had come out of the foliage, and were standing in front of them, staring at them as if they were some kind of strange animal. The Spaniards realized that this was probably the native's first encounter with white men, since it was theirs with the Indians. The leader of their group, Sergeant Luis Tiante, locked hands and forearms with each of his own men, as was the European custom of greeting a friend and comrade, and then embraced them as friends; he then stepped forward, smiled, and offered his hand to one of the Indians. The most decorated of the group walked up to him and tentatively offered his hand to the Sergeant. They joined hands and arms together, and the Indian began doing the same with each of the sailors. The other Indians followed suit, and everything appeared to be friendly.

None of the Indians spoke any Spanish; it was known that the priests of Saint Augustine to the north, like the Spanish priests everywhere across New Spain, had taught some of the Indians to speak elementary Spanish, but apparently they hadn't gotten to this region so far south. So the Sergeant and the Indians developed a quick form of rudimentary communication by pointing out things and saying the word in Spanish, or in the Indians' native tongue.

They were able to enlist the help of these local Indians, a tribe that called themselves the *Ais*. After their initial meeting at the spring, the Indians had come out to the beach and had assisted the Spaniards in establishing their camp. They showed the men how to catch fish at the river mouth, and provided wild boar and venison for the mess tables. They showed them how to dig clams in the sand, and how to collect oysters from the shallow waters on the west side of the island. They took the men to a freshwater spring hidden in the dense jungle just a short distance from their camp; the Spaniards who had gone out in search of water had never found it, and probably never would have, without the Indians' help.

But their biggest contribution came when Captain de Avila found out that they were accomplished swimmers, and that they were willing to work on the wrecks just off the shore. Their skills quickly paid off; they continued to bring up baskets of treasure and supplies, handing them off to men in the longboats or the large floating rafts that the Spaniards had put together for the salvage work. At the end of each day, the Captain would give each of the Indian divers a silver coin from the treasure trove. Word spread through the tribe that a shiny silver piece was the reward for helping the Spaniards, and each day more of the Indians showed up for work.

The salvage effort continued for weeks before a longboat appeared on the beach near their encampment. Captain de Avila had men watching the coastline for ships, and seeing a large galleon just offshore that was flying the Spanish flag they had built a huge bonfire, alerting the ship of their presence. The Captain of the galleon had sent a small group of his marines in the longboat to establish who the signalers were; upon seeing that they were part of the missing treasure fleet, they brought Captain de Avila back to the ship with them.

Captain de Avila was greeted warmly by the Captain and his crew. They went to the Captain's quarters, where they enjoyed a meal and some Jamaican rum. He told the Captain and his officers about the storm that had destroyed the fleet, and his efforts to retrieve the sunken treasures for King Felipe'.

Captain Don Francisco Montoya, captain of the galleon, had sailed south from Saint Augustine as part of the original protection group, but as the seas picked up just before the *huracana*, his group was able to get into a safe harbor along the coast. Of the four ships, his was the only one that survived the storm with minimal damage. The others had been able to get back to the garrison and were in port being repaired, but would soon be ready to sail again. The Governor at Saint Augustine had ordered him to sail south again in search of the fleet, and to assist with whatever needed to be done to help in their efforts.

After their stories were told, the two Captains decided that it would be best if Captain Montoya would sail to Havana to raise the ships and men that it would take to finish the job that the survivors and the Indians had begun. He would return as quickly as possible to evacuate the men and the treasure, and the precious cargo would be part of another flotilla leaving in September for Spain. King Felipe' needed the treasure more than ever.

CHAPTER 38

Savannah, Georgia
December 14th, 1977

I WAS coming out of the Piggly Wiggly Supermarket at the end of my shift when I was approached by a couple of rough looking men. They stopped about twenty feet in front of me, and just stood and glared. I wasn't sure what they wanted, but I was pretty certain they weren't locals; they had the hardened look of some of the boys that worked for my father back in Boston. I knew the look; they were a mix of corned beef, potatoes and beer, and a lot of street nasty to go with the rest. As we stood looking at each other for what felt like an hour, I was beginning to feel that this wasn't going to be good. These boys weren't here to talk; they had been looking for me, and they got what they wanted.

"Do I know you guys?" I asked. "Something I can do for you?" I continued our stand-off, praying that some people would come out from the store and distract my new friends long enough for me to run. My prayers went unanswered, though, and the parking lot seemed as empty as a bottle of Jameson's at closing time.

The bigger one of the two finally spoke up and answered that they were in town looking for an old friend from Boston, and that I sure looked just like him.

"His name is Jackie Burke, and I swear you look just like him! You could be his twin, but I'm a very good friend of his father's, and I know that there isn't a twin in the family anywhere. I even went to the boy's christening, so, you see, I would know if there was two of him. I know that my friend Big John would find it funny as hell to know that his boy's got a look-alike, all the way down here in Savannah, Georgia. Your name tag says your name's *Don*, but you sure do look like Jackie. Maybe you can tell us where you're from, lad?"

"I'm from New York, originally, but my parents were both killed in a bad car accident. I came down here to live with some family. I'm sorry I can't help you find your friend, good luck with that!"

As I walked to the right, away from the two thugs, I sensed that they were circling around me. Not knowing what might come next, but knowing that it wouldn't be good, I broke into a sprint, heading for the middle of the parking lot. The lot was full of cars, and would offer me some cover. "Where the hell was everybody?" I thought, still hoping for a last-minute rush of shoppers to aid my retreat. Maybe I could lose these guys in the maze, maybe not, but I knew that I needed to try and the time was now.

As soon as I started running, I heard the matching footsteps of the two men pursuing me; they were both big men, surprisingly faster than I thought they'd be, and I couldn't seem to shake them. I thought I was gaining ground on them, since I had got the jump on them, but just when I felt that freedom was mine, I felt a white-hot pain in my left arm. Unable to catch me, the big man had shot me and yelled out to me as I kept putting distance between us. "That one's from Big John, boy! He still owes you an arse whipping, and there's no place you can hide. We'll find you again, Jackie boy!"

CHAPTER 39

The San Sebastian Treasure Museum
Sebastian Inlet, Florida, October 10th, 2004

"THE Spanish Admiral sent a recovery fleet from Havana, Cuba, only days after the Captain of the search ship showed up. Upon learning of the treasure that had been saved, he knew it was the most important order of business that he get the reclaimed riches to King Felipe'. The King would be very disappointed to learn that so much wealth was at the bottom of the sea floor, but the Admiral could do nothing to prevent what had happened. Showing the King that he had recovered at least part of the treasure was something that he hoped Felipe' could be grateful for. Does anyone have any questions about any of this?"

"Yes, Miss Morgan, how much of the original treasure was recovered by the Spaniards?"

"Please, call me Sue. It's estimated that only about 25% of what left Havana was found by the Spaniards and their Indian divers. The rest remained behind, swallowed up by the reefs and shifting sands of this stretch of coastline. No one is certain exactly where all of the ships went down, but the majority of the discoveries have come within the three counties here. That's why today, this entire area, from Stuart to Sebastian Inlet, is called the Treasure Coast. The name was adopted by the local Chambers of Commerce to enhance the area's popularity."

"Are people still finding treasure here, after all these years?"

"Amazingly so; in fact, Sebastian has a small group of treasure salvagers that work off the beaches here every summer when the winds calm down. The sands give up rich prizes year after year, which keeps the pros and amateurs alike coming back to search again. After a big storm, you can see dozens of people walking the beaches with metal detectors, looking for that elusive piece of gold or silver. Just last year, a man working a detector on the beach in front of the *Disney Resort* south of here found a clump of gold coins that were stuck together with skeletal coral. It was incredible!"

"Who was the first to start salvaging these wrecks?"

"Well, nobody knows the real answer to that; it's been rumored for many years that a small group of local men up and down the coast had been diving on the old wrecks, and had been very successful in finding quite a bit of gold and silver coins. It's unknown how much these men had recovered, but it seems that each of them led a much richer lifestyle in their later years. A Vero Beach man, Kip Wagner, was one of the earliest salvagers to officially work the wrecks. He and his divers found quite a bit of treasure and artifacts, many of which are part of our collection here at the museum.

As to the professionals, though, there is one company that has the Federal and State salvage rights to all of the Treasure Coast, and any companies that want to work the wrecks have to go through them to get permission. Any valuables found are then shared with the State of Florida and the salvage master. That's actually how we've gotten so many great historical items here in the Museum. Because we're run by the State, we get to share the bounty. It's been a great association for all of us involved."

"How do you know so much about all of this? Did you grow up in the area?"

"No, actually, I grew up in Kansas. I joined the Coast Guard when I got out of high school, did my four years, and began my new life. I was working for UPS, as a driver and packer, making pretty good money, when Uncle Sam called to invite me back into the Coast Guard. There was a war in the Middle East, as you know, and the Government was calling up Reservists all around the country to man stations that were short of personnel. I ended up stationed in Fort Pierce, just south of here. Living in the middle of the Treasure Coast, it didn't take long before I heard the stories of sunken treasure. I was hooked! I was already a certified scuba diver, so I looked into getting a job as a treasure hunter as soon as my time was up. I came to Sebastian, joined up with one of the dive companies, and started working. I did that for several years, and I loved it! We were constantly finding things; not all gold and silver, but historical pieces, too. It was fun; I don't think I was ever happier."

"Then why aren't you still diving?"

"A few years ago, after having a serious blackout while diving, I found out that I had a problem with my heart. It wasn't enough to kill me if I didn't put a strain on it, but I had to give up diving. I heard about this job at the Museum, and applied for it the same day. They liked the fact that I was an actual treasure diver and knew so much about the fleet, and they called me right away. They offered me the job, and I accepted it before I even knew how much it paid, but it's kept me involved with the treasure hunting and the history, so I'm pretty happy with the way it turned out."

CHAPTER 40

Sebastian, Florida
October 12th, 2004

R AY Eldridge had stopped drinking beer the day he pulled CJ out of the water. Now he started every day with a shot or two of Tequila, followed by a few hits of weed. The days that followed CJ's death had been as ugly as Ray had ever known, and beer just wouldn't cut through that feeling. The tequila usually had him pretty drunk by mid-afternoon, and today was no different.

He was sitting at the bar in *Suzy's Tiki Bar*, a little local spot on Indian River Drive. He had tied up his boat here after bringing CJ in, and the owners had been nice enough to just let him leave it there. He hadn't been out, or even started it; it just reminded him of that awful day. But today, he was talking to some guy that worked for some local treasure salvage company. The guy was drunk like him, and was rambling on about all the shit they'd found after the storms. He said that the hurricanes had ripped up the beaches pretty bad, and that they had un-covered all kinds of stuff from some 'Plate Fleet', or some-thing like that.

The gold chain that CJ had brought up just before all hell broke loose flashed into his soggy mind. He had forgotten about it after everything that had happened! The sparkling vision came into focus in his head, and he couldn't believe that he hadn't remembered it before now. Holy Shit! He realized that he'd been so drunk since CJ died, that the chain had gone right out his window! What a dumbshit!

"What'd you say about that plate thing?"

Ray's new-found friend, eager to expound on his knowledge, was quick to give Ray some schoolin'. "It's called *The 1715 Plate Fleet*, and its remains are scattered all over the beaches and reefs along the coast. Christ, don't you know why they call this The Treasure Coast? It's because of all that shit that them sunken ships left all over the place. Didn't you say you grew up here?"

"Yeah, I did, but I guess I forgot about the treasure shit. My father took me to the museum over on the beach when I was a kid, but I ain't talked about it in years. Why they call it a Plate Fleet, were there plates, or treasures on these boats?"

"That's pretty funny, man. There was a bunch of real plates on some of the ships; they had been shipped from China to Mexico, and were being sent to the King in Spain. The real reason it's called the Plate Fleet, though, is because of the silver coins on board every ship. The silver coins were called 'platas' by the Spanish, which eventually became translated as 'plates' in English. That's why it's the Plate Fleet, man."

"Well, shit, I didn't know that. That's pretty interesting stuff."

"Well, hell ya man, it's pretty cool. I been divin' with this crew for most of the past ten years, and we find some pretty good shit out there every year. Usually, we're done for the season by now, because the ocean's too riled up this time of year, but we're finding stuff inside the Lagoon and on the beaches that's washed up after the storms. It's freakin' unbelievable!"

"Yeah, sounds cool, man."

Ray's mind, at least what was left of it, began to spin. The gold chain must be part of that treasure this guy's talking about. He began to form a plan to go find that chain; he knew that CJ would want him to have it. Hell, that would keep him in Tequila and weed for a long damned time, that's for sure!

But, as he started thinking about finding the chain, Ray's mind flashed back to CJ in the water, and that God-awful scream that he let out just before he was pulled under. Shit, he thought, would it even be worth it, taking a risk that could end up killing him just like his old buddy. And then it hit him!

"Hey, bud, what's your name?"

"Eric Trombley, dude. What's yours?"

"It's Ray; Ray Eldridge. It's funny how I seen ya in here before, but didn't ever ask your name. Funny how, sometimes, it just don't matter, ya know? We're just two guys in here killing a drink or two, that's all."

"Yeah, I hear you, man. You're right about not givin' a shit sometimes."

"Yeah. Listen, Eric, are you the kind of guy that might like a little adventure making some money?"

"I'm definitely not interested in runnin' drugs, if

that's what you're talkin' about, but I do like a good opportunity, brother."

"Well, I got a proposal for ya, but it's gotta be just between you and me. Nobody else can know, or I'd have to kill ya, as they say. If you're interested in hearin' about it, let's take a walk out on the dock. My boat's out there; I need to take it for a quick run. You in?"

"Let's do it, dude. What have ya got goin' on?"

"We'll talk about it on the way; that way, I'll have your complete attention, know what I mean?"

Ray and Eric jumped into the skiff tied up at the end of the dock. It took a few cranks to get it going, but as always, the motor turned over, and off they went. Ray told the new guy about the fateful day that CJ found the chain, and told him how it was probably a big shark that had wandered in from the beachside. A1A had been repaired, and once again, was being used as always, so the chances of a big shark being in that area were probably slim to none, as they say. They had agreed that Eric, a diver by trade, would search for the chain, and that Ray would work the boat. Eric knew where to get rid of the treasure, although it wasn't necessarily the *legal* scenario. Ray had offered to give him a 25% share for doing the diving and the sale. Eric thought that since he was taking all the chances that he should get 50%; they argued about it for a few minutes and settled on a 60/40 split. As they approached the area, Ray slowed the boat.

He started to make slow circles, reminding him, of course, of the circles he had made looking for CJ. He knew that he was in the right area; he'd never forget that spot. Thirty minutes passed, and they saw nothing shiny anywhere. They decided to make one more loop, and Ray steered the boat back into the center of the circle, where they had started. Standing up on the bow, Eric shouted that he thought he saw something shiny, and Ray should stop the boat. Ray's heart was beating so hard that he thought his head would explode! Could this be what he came for; what his friend died for? It was time to find out.

As they came up on the shiny object, Eric dove in. He came up a minute later with the gold chain; he was holding it by what looked to be some kind of head. Ray came closer, and saw that it was the head of a snake, and it was damned ugly! But the chain had to be at least six foot long, made of heavy links; it was covered with all kinds of shit, but to Ray and Eric, it was the most beautiful thing they'd ever seen!

Ray gave Eric a hand getting back into the boat; expecting the same fate as CJ, Ray tensed, wondering if anything was going to happen. As Eric stood up in the boat, they both began to laugh. They had found a treasure that was certainly worth a ton of money, and nothing bad had happened.

"Holy shit, we did it" exclaimed Ray. He and Eric gave each other *high 5's*, whooping it up in the middle of the boat. Ray was so happy that he gave Eric a bear hug like he'd only ever given his best friend CJ. It was a great feeling!

The intensity of the hit they took next knocked both of them out of the boat, and into the water. It had felt like a bulldozer had hit them, but neither one of them had seen it coming. As he struggled to get himself right, Ray sensed a great power in the water with him. He couldn't see anything, but he just knew it was there. He didn't see Eric, either, and wondered if he was still alive, because Ray already knew that the chances of them making it out of here alive weren't very good.

He found the side of his boat, and pulled himself up out of the water. Not seeing Eric anywhere, Ray hit the throttle and got out of there as fast as his boat would fly. Looking back later, Ray thought that maybe his boat realized how much trouble they were in, and went faster than he ever remembered. Whatever, he just got his ass gone!

CHAPTER 41

Sebastian Inlet State Park, South Park
October 12th, 2004

MARK Thomas had watched the boat with the two fishermen on it as they had pulled into the area south of the park a couple days earlier. He thought that they were fishing, because he had seen the one guy, Ray *'something'*, out fishing off the Inlet with his buddy, the first guy that got killed. Mark was a Park Ranger there for many years, so he knew most of the regulars that worked the waters around the Park.

He was making his normal rounds, and had stopped to watch some fish that were smashing a mullet school just off the beach. They were probably jacks, but it was always fun to watch them *seek & destroy* the way that they did; the way they cornered the bait pods was a thing of beauty, an act of survival. He was about to get back into his truck to head over to the north side when he saw Ray's boat slide into the area just south of him.

Thinking it odd that Ray was back in the same area where his best friend had been killed, he decided to stay for a few extra minutes. Ray had the boat going in circles, like he was looking for something. He continued making loops for close to a half hour, then stopped the boat. The other guy with him, a man he thought he had seen around the park, went over the side into the water.

A couple of minutes passed before he saw the swimmer raising something shiny over his head. Since he was a couple hundred yards away, he really couldn't tell what it was from the beach, but guessed that it must be something worthwhile. "Why the hell would Ray go back there so soon after his friend got killed? That would be pretty stupid", he thought; then he remembered that neither one of those boys had been admired for their intelligence. They were, as the locals liked to say, just a couple of *fumducks*!

The new guy got up into the boat, and he and Ray started hugging like a couple of schoolgirls. "What the hell?" As he watched the dancing, he thought he saw something come out of the water. Whatever it was, it was powerful enough to knock both of the men into the water. It had happened so fast that it wasn't more than a blur from where he was, but he was sure he had seen something.

Seeing the water churned up pretty good around the boat, Mike continued to watch. He saw one of the men crawl up over the gunnels into the boat. It was Ray, and he had started the motor up. Taking one glance around him, he fired that boat out of there as fast as he could, heading back toward Sebastian.

"What the hell? Where was the other guy, and what had just happened?" He stood motionless, as his eyes scanned the water south of him; he saw nothing moving.

Nothing; as in no birds, no fish, no breeze, just nothing! "It was weirder than shit," he thought. Feeling as if he needed to do something, Mark called out to a fisherman coming up to the ramp in his boat.

"Hey, I need to use your boat for an emergency", he yelled, "I think there might be a problem out there."

"Well, jump in, and I'll go with you. No offense, man, but I don't want you, or anybody else, taking off with my boat!"

"Okay, but let's go now; we need to get down there as soon as we can!"

The two of them headed south, away from the ramp. They were the only ones around, since it was a weekday, so getting off quickly wasn't an issue. As they approached the area west of Ambersand, where he had seen the trouble, Mark told the driver to slow up.

"What are we looking for, Ranger?"

Not wanting to alarm the fisherman too much, and not really sure that he wanted to tell him everything anyhow, Mark told him that he had seen a disturbance in the water, and that he might have seen a person in the water. "I'm not sure", he said flatly, "I just want to check, is all."

He told the man to circle around this area slowly, to see if they could spot something, or somebody, in the water. He was searching east of the boat, and the driver was looking west. As they drove along slowly, he caught a flash on the bottom. "Holy shit", he thought, "it's something gold! It must be part of the lost treasure!"

Mark made a quick visual reconnaissance; he noted the spot as best he could, using local landmarks and an old tree submerged in the muck. He sure as hell wasn't telling this guy about the gold, no matter what; he'd come back on his own for that when the time was right.

"I guess I must have seen some dolphin chasing bait, or something else. Let's head back in; sorry to have got you involved. It must have been the sun in my eyes, or something."

"That's no problem, I'm glad to help!" The man turned his boat back to the ramp, where Mark tied the boat up to the dock, and jumped into his truck.

"Thanks for your help! Sorry it was just a false alarm; have a good day!" Mark called out as he drove away. He'd be back again for that shiny thing out there, but first he had to figure out what happened to the swimmer who had come up with the gold, and who seemed to have vanished. He was gonna have to think this one over, and get out there before Ray made another attempt. Right now it was a race to see who gets the prize, and he had never been one to lose at much. He'd figure it out, but it might take some time. He chuckled to himself that he might have all the time in the World; the way that Ray had gotten out of there made him think that it might be a long while before he'd go back to that little patch of sea grass.

CHAPTER 42

Monster Hole, Sebastian Inlet
October 14th, 2004

THERE had been a big storm offshore for days, coming up out of the Bahamas, and it had been stirring up some big surf along the East Coast of Florida. The weathermen had said that this might be the last big disturbance of the season, so anybody who could take the time, and who had a board, was out in the surf taking advantage of the six to eight footers rolling in. For years, Sebastian Inlet, and especially Monster Hole, on the south side, was the hot spot for the best surfers. All of the big names on the Pro Tour had surfed here, and a tour event was held here every year. So it was no surprise that dozens of surfers were riding the swells, hoping for a better ride than the last one.

Ronny Smith, a long time surfer, had grown up in Florida with a board under one arm, and a fishing rod in the other. He was like hundreds of kids, living for the ride, and he wouldn't miss the Monster Hole waves for anything. He was there with his buddy, Brian Clancy, and the two of them were having an incredible day. The waves were coming in one after another, all of them so good it was almost difficult to choose one and go. The boys couldn't remember a day like this in years; it couldn't get any better, they thought.

As they sat on their boards, waiting for the next big wave, something bumped against Ronny's leg. He instinctively pulled both of his feet out of the water, and told Brian to do the same. He began yelling to other surfers around him that there might be a shark in the water, and to be careful.

As his eyes peered into the water below him, he saw a flash of red, and what he thought might be khaki. Red and khaki? He knew that what he was seeing wasn't a shark, but a person, who had obviously drowned. He told Brian what he saw, and jumped off his board. Swimming to the red, he grabbed onto a t-shirt, and swam back up. Getting onto his board, he hung onto the corpse, and started paddling into shore. Brian followed him, and they both hit the beach together. They pulled the body out of the surf, and dropped it onto the beach. Their faces froze as they saw the body of a man with his chest ripped open.

Mark Thomas was in the Ranger Station when the telephone rang. Ron Krieger, another Ranger, was on the desk; he picked up the phone to take the call. He listened to the caller, then got off the phone. Even before he had hung up, he was telling Mark they needed to get over to the South Beach, at the Monster Hole. Two surfers had just pulled a body out of the waves, and it wasn't good. The caller had said that the man's chest had been torn up by sharks, or something, and that it was pretty gory.

The two men jumped in the Park truck, and headed

out of the station. They crossed over A1A to the beachside, where they switched the truck over to four wheel drive and headed out onto the sands. There was a large crowd of surfers and beach-goers all gathered around, gawking at the body lying on the sand.

"Did anyone call the Sheriff's Department about this?" Mark asked, as the two of them made their way into the crowd.

Somebody yelled out that they had called them first, and then called the Rangers. The dispatcher had said that they'd get somebody out there as quickly as possible, but had suggested that they call the Ranger Station. The distant sound of a siren told them that a Deputy would probably be here soon.

The two kids who had pulled the body out of the surf were standing over it, as if it was some kind of prize. They probably figured that this would be on television that night, and they didn't want to give up their *fifteen minutes of fame* that everyone hears about. Why else would they want to be around this corpse? It was the most gruesome thing that anyone on the beach had ever seen, but it seemed to hold everyone's attention the way a really bad car wreck does. "There's a name for that," thought Mark.

A big man in a green Sheriff's uniform came running down the beach. He started clearing people out as soon as he got close; he was the first officer 'on scene', and he needed to make sure that he followed official protocol. As he backed people off the body, he took his first look at the victim. Being new to the department, the Deputy had encountered something like this only one other time, and it was just a few days ago; he had to hold on to his stomach, as the bile rose in his throat. This body looked just like the other one last week, and he knew that something about this wasn't right!

Mark Thomas saw the red t-shirt and the khaki shorts on the man. He knew who it was without taking his fingerprints; it was the swimmer from Ray's boat. Now he had his answer; two men who had gone in the water after the golden treasure had met the same gruesome fate. He wasn't going to be the next victim; he had to figure out a way to get that thing out of the water without going in. The wheels in his head started spinning as he walked back to the truck.

CHAPTER 43

Vero Lake Estates
October 15th, 2004

THE phone in the kitchen kept ringing. It wouldn't stop; every couple of minutes it would start ringing again. Ray was in bed with a huge hangover. He'd tied up the boat at Suzy's, drove 'Jeanne' home, and had been drunk ever since. He hadn't told anyone about what happened with Eric, and nobody had even noticed that he was alone when he tied the boat up. Some band was playing, and everybody was busy getting drunk, so he just left without talking to anyone.

The ringing was about to cause his head to come off, so he dragged himself out of bed, and headed for the kitchen. It wasn't ringing right now, so he poured himself a shot, and sat down at the table. As the Tequila started to work itself into his throbbing head, the phone started ringing again. It was CJ's old lady Esther.

"Ray, where the hell you been? I've been trying to get you for two hours!"

"Oh, Mrs. Hilton, I'm sorry about that. I must have been out in the barn."

"I doubt that, Ray. You probably either been getting drunk, or sleeping one off."

"Yes, ma'am, you're right about that. What can I do for you?"

"You can't do nothing, Ray. I just wanted to tell you that some surfer kid found another body with its heart missing; chewed out just like my boy CJ. I can't believe it, Ray. Two people with the same horrible death; what the hell we gonna do, Ray?"

As Esther Hilton prattled on, the doorbell on the front door starting ringing. "Jesus", he thought, "what now?"

"Mrs. Hilton, I gotta go; somebody's ringing my doorbell now. Nobody wants me to get any sleep today. I'll stop by next week to see you."

"Yeah, sure, Ray. Just like the last time. Good bye!"

The doorbell rang again. He grabbed his shorts, slid into them, and grabbed a clean T-shirt. After pulling it on, he opened his front door. Two men, who identified themselves as detectives from the Indian River County Sheriff's Department, asked if they could come in.

"Well, sure, what's this all about?"

The larger of the two men, Detective Alex Brown, was the first to speak. "We'd like to talk to you about a body that was found just outside the Inlet yesterday."

"Why would you want to talk to me?"

The other detective, Paul Williams, answered quickly (too quickly, Ray thought). "The body looked just like your friend CJ's, with its chest ripped open. And somebody said that they saw you leave the bar with this guy in your boat, and then saw you come back alone later. Kind of a coincidence, Mr. Eldridge, that you were present when both of these men lost their lives? The man's name was Eric Trombley; does that mean anything to you, sir?"

"Uh, yeah. I was talking with this guy, and he says he needs a ride back to the Inlet Campground. I figure, what the hell? It's a great day for a boat ride, so I gave him a ride over to the Park. No big deal; I haven't seen him since."

"Some kids surfing outside the Inlet found his body floating. The Coroner says it's hard to figure time of death, because of him being in the water, but he thinks that it was probably sometime in the last few days. Since you were seen with him on the 12th, it was obviously between then and now. Can you give us any help here, Mr. Eldridge?"

"Well, you probably know the guy was a diver; he worked for some treasure company here. They were working over by the Inlet; maybe he got attacked by a shark like CJ did."

"Maybe that's what happened, or maybe not. You think of anything, you call us, okay?"

"Yeah, sure, but I don't think I can help you with anything. Have a nice day, Detectives."

The call from Mrs. Hilton, and the detectives showing up, had damned near caused Ray to soil his britches. Holy Christ! I'm in a bucket of shit, he thought. His hand went to the tequila bottle, and he sucked down a long swig of the golden nectar. It will be okay, he told himself as the alcohol hit his stomach. No problem.

CHAPTER 44

Sebastian Inlet State Park
October 16th, 2004

THE day after Ray Eldridge was being questioned by the Sheriff's Detectives, Mark Thomas was backing his boat down the ramp at the Inlet. He'd thought long and hard about the shiny gold thing in the water, and how he was going to get it before Ray showed up again. It looked like some kind of rope, or chain, so he had come up with a way to salvage it. The water was the secret; both of the men who had died had gone into the water to retrieve the chain. He wasn't about to make the same mistake.

His son, Sean, had taken the day off as he had told him to, and was in the boat with him now. He had filled Sean in on the previous events, but had assured him that he could get this done without injury to either one of them. As he approached the spot where the treasure lay on the bottom, Mark switched out places with his son, having Sean take over the boat. He got out one of his offshore trolling rods, a real stiff one, with fifty pound braided line, and showed Sean the weighted treble hook he had tied on the end. All he had to do was locate the item, drop the leaded hook overboard, and try to snag the chain with it. Once he did that, he told Sean "don't look back, just get our asses outta here as fast as you can!"

Sean proceeded very slowly through the area, helping his Dad look for the shiny gold chain. After about fifteen minutes, he spotted it, lying in four feet of water, partly tangled in the grass bed below. "Dad, I got it! It's right over here; I'm almost on top of it."

Mark came over to the starboard side, where Sean stood, and peered into the water. His polarized glasses cut through the glare, and he too saw the thing that they had come for. It was a chain, and it was huge! "Oh my God, son, do you see how big that thing is? It's incredible!"

"Dad, are you sure that your rig will work? It's only in a few feet, and I can get it in no time."

"Son, there's no friggin' way you're getting in that water! Just get the boat moving forward, and give me a minute to latch on to that thing."

Sean inched the boat forward, driving right over the top of the chain; he put the boat into neutral and drifted, as his father dropped the hook into the water.

"Shit!" Mark had missed on the first swing, and wasn't eager to try again; he knew that there was something bad going on out here, and he wanted to be long gone before anything happened. "Take another pass by; I'll get it this time. Be ready to haul ass!"

Sean swung the boat around slowly, and brought it back over the chain. Mark saw it, and dropped his hook into the grass. He tugged gently, and felt the weight of the chain on the end of his line. "Alright, hit it, and get the hell outta here! I got it."

Sean threw the boat into gear, and buried it. The boat was coming up on plane in seconds, and his Dad had the chain. "We're gonna get this damned thing; Dad was right," he thought.

Mark was holding on for dear life, not wanting to lose his treasure. Facing the rear of the boat, he was trying to reel the chain in, but it seemed that it was gaining weight, becoming heavier and heavier. He was struggling with it, like it was a fifty pound amberjack. He tightened down on his drag, and kept reeling. He had to get this thing in; Sean was really getting the boat cranked up.

Suddenly the line went almost slack; there was barely any pressure on it, and it felt like a fish that was running at you faster than you could reel. Mark saw something coming up in the water behind the boat, and he started thinking that this wasn't good. Not good at all!

He started reeling as hard as he could. The gold was all he could think about; they were almost a quarter mile away from the site, and he needed to get that thing into the boat. Time was running out, and he was sure that he might lose the chain if Sean got the boat up to top speed once he got it into the channel. Sweat was pouring out of him like he'd never sweat before, and he was worried that this wasn't going as well as he planned. He leaned in and gave the rod a pull, and started reeling faster.

Something that Mark couldn't have dreamed about in his worst nightmare came flying out of the water behind him, and hit him with enough force to knock him out cold. His body dropped to the deck with a thud, and

Sean cut the motor and turned around to find out what was going on. What he saw froze him to the deck.

There was something that looked like a huge snake in the back of the boat, and it was hovering over his father as he watched every move that Sean made. The serpent's head was huge, and it seemed to be golden in color; the body was a metallic green, glistening in the sun. Its eyes were the most evil thing that Sean had ever seen, and they were firmly planted on him. Without warning, the snake tore into his father's chest, and savagely ripped his heart out.

The serpent was holding his father's heart in his teeth. Blood was dripping from its mouth, and its evil eyes had turned into liquid fire. Sean felt the warm trickle of piss running down his legs, but he couldn't move. It was the last thing Sean remembered, as the serpent hit him head on, just like he had done to Mark.

Capt. Bill Stoddard was on his way back to Sebastian after taking five guys from Orlando out bottom fishing all day. They had gotten a box full, too, and everyone was pretty happy, especially since most of them were working on their second six-pack of the day. He had gone under the A1A Bridge, heading west, when he saw a boat floating in the current just off the southern tip of the park. The boat appeared to be empty; he couldn't believe that anyone would be dumb enough to dive in the Inlet channel, and he didn't see a dive flag, anyhow. With no storms around, and hardly any wind, he thought "what the hell was a boat doing out here by itself?"

A couple of the less drunk fishermen on board spotted the boat, and asked him what was up with the empty boat?

"Not sure; I'll know better when I come up on it in a couple minutes. It might just have cut loose from somebody's dock, or maybe it floated up off the beach over at the park."

Capt. Bill made his way to the drifting boat. He thought that he could see something in the boat, but he wasn't sure; he'd be on it in a minute, and then he could figure it out. As he got closer, he started calling out for the captain, or anyone else on board. He cut his engines as he started coming up on the boat. He asked one of his guests to grab his long handled boat hook, and asked him to try to grab the side of the boat.

One of the other anglers yelled out "Holy shit! Look at that!" He leaned over the side of the boat, and began throwing up everywhere. The rest of the guys all saw what he had seen, and joined him in chucking up their guts. Capt. Bill and his mate, who hadn't been drinking all day, did everything that they could to not join the rest of the crew, but it was impossible. They, too, lost it over the rail.

The bodies of Mark and Sean Thomas lay in bloody heaps at both ends of the boat. Blood was everywhere, and both men had had their chests ripped open; it was the worst thing that any of them had ever seen.

Capt. Bill called it into the Coast Guard; he didn't know what else to do.

CHAPTER 45

Vero Lake Estates
October 17, 2004

R AY Eldridge was having breakfast when he heard
something on the radio about two bodies that had
been found drifting in a boat out by the Inlet yesterday.
He choked on a mouthful of scrambled eggs as he listened to the news reporter talking about the discovery.
The newsman was saying that an informed source close
to the investigation had told him that the two mutilated
corpses resembled those of two other local men whose
bodies had been found in the water near the Inlet recently. He added that the Indian River County Sheriff's Department had asked the State Police for help in solving
what was now starting to look like something out of a
Stephen King novel.

The announcer went on to say that the police weren't
giving out the names of the latest victims, but it was believed to be a father and son who had gone out fishing.
Even though there was no fishing gear on board, it was
assumed to be a fishing trip, since the father, it was being
rumored, was a ranger out at the Inlet Park, and he and

his son had been fishing out there many times.

"Son of a bitch!" Ray thought. "This guy must have seen me out there with Eric; he must have seen what happened, and went exploring. Christ! This is unbelievable."

Ray hadn't had a drink yet, but decided that now was a good time to start. He had been trying to slow up on the liquor the last couple of days, but the news today was a good enough reason to crack open the bottle. He grabbed his bottle of tequila, the latest one, and unscrewed the top. He stared into the bottle for a minute, and put it back down on the table. "God, this ain't what I need to do. I gotta stop whatever's goin' on out there, but I can't do it alone. I gotta go see Cap'n Don; he'll know what to do," he thought to himself, as he twisted the top of the tequila bottle back on.

CHAPTER 46

Miami, Florida
December 19th, 1977

"**H**ow old are you, son?""I've just turned eighteen, sir, a few months ago."

"Okay, do you have some formal identification like a License or a passport?"

I had gotten my wound cleaned and stitched up by a cousin of Charlotte's who was attending med school. It was a clean through shot, and hadn't done much damage, but it continued to throb worse than anything I'd ever gone through. I had told Charlotte everything about my previous life in Boston, right down to the story of the 'carjacking gone bad'. I had also told her that I needed to leave Savannah just as quickly as I could, and waiting around for me might not be a good idea. She didn't seem to have any problem with that; after hearing my sordid tale, she couldn't have been less interested in me. So we hugged and said goodbye, and I never saw her again.

Once again, I boarded a Greyhound bus heading south. Miami was the last stop, so that's where I went. Along the way, I had decided that joining the military might be the right thing to do; it would take me out of the limelight for a few years, and hopefully, it would be safer for everybody.

While taking a little bus tour of Miami after I arrived, I found myself going over the Miami River. There were Coast Guard boats in the river, and they looked pretty cool. While in Savannah, I had gone out several times with Charlotte's father in his forty-eight foot sport-fisherman, and found that I loved being out on the water. "What the hell?" I thought. "I'll join the Coast Guard, and maybe they can put me somewhere far from Boston."

But I had never thought about verifying who I was to anybody. My assumed identity had worked for me for a while, and I thought that I could continue to be Don Buckley, of Savannah, Georgia. Now, here I was, sitting in front of this Coast Guard recruiter, and I didn't even have any proof of who I was. I decided to trust the man, and told him everything about my recent past in an effort to make him understand my circumstances.

The recruiter chuckled and told me that I wouldn't be the first person to join the military to get away from an ugly past. "Before you left Boston did you ever get a Social Security number?"

"Yes sir, I did. My mother had gotten me one when I was young. I know the number; it's the only thing I've got."

"Well, as a member of the United States military, I am able to pull some strings in Washington to get some answers, so give me your number and I'll do some checking. It takes the government a little time to respond, so why don't you come back on Friday, and we'll see if we can't take care of this for you?"

"That would be great, sir. Here's my number." I wrote my Social Security number down for the man and said goodbye, thanking him on my way out the door.

On Friday morning, I was back at the Recruiting Station. The officer that I had spoken to smiled when I came in, and I thought that seemed like a good sign.

"Well, good morning, Don. I thought I might see you early today. I've got good news for you; I was able to confirm your Social Security number to verify your date of birth. We can finish those enlistment papers if you still want to go ahead with joining the Coast Guard. And, you can use the name Don Buckley, if you'd like. You'll need to go see a friend of mine downtown; he's a paralegal who can make your name change official. There won't be a problem with anything."

"Excellent, sir, let's get this done!"

The man pulled out my file and started putting pages in front of me. "Just sign here, here and here, and we're done."

I signed the three places the man had marked, and handed the forms back to him.

The recruiter looked everything over a final time and closed the file. "Welcome to the United States Coast Guard, Don Buckley! Here's the address of my friend's office; he's expecting you."

CHAPTER 47

Miami, Florida
January 3rd, 1978

I REPORTED for duty at the Miami Coast Guard Station; they were going to send me to San Diego, California, for training first, and then would assign me to a station someplace in the States. I didn't care where, as long as it wasn't in the Northeast.

I finished my training, and true to their word, the Coast Guard sent me to Seattle, Washington, for my first posting. In addition to my normal duties, I started studying to get my Captain's License; although I knew it might be a long shot, I dreamed about driving the Coastie boats that I crewed on. I earned my *six-pack* license first, and then I signed up for my 100 Ton Master's License. To get that license, I had to literally work on a qualifying boat, earning my required hours as a mate. That had to be done on my own hours, so I never wasted a minute of free time. I befriended an old tug boat captain, who needed some help with his driving. It seemed that the old man was a drinker, so letting me drive his boat whenever I was available made perfectly good sense. After a year, I had the required hours, and I passed the test for my new license.

My friends in the Coast Guard had become calling me *Captain Don* after I completed my Masters License. The name stuck, and I eventually accepted it as my *nom de guerre,* or so I liked to call it. From that time on, everybody I met along the way just called me Captain Don.

My four years in the Coast Guard passed quickly, and I enjoyed every minute of it. I spent time in Galveston, Texas, Biloxi, Mississippi, back to San Diego, and did two tours in Antarctica, on a duty that the Coast Guard called *Operation Deepfreeze,* a six month long effort to keep the ice broken up so that ships could get to the expeditionary bases scattered amongst the ice.

I got to drive the boats, too. Every chance I got, I would jump on a boat to drive. By the time my tour was up, I had captained almost every boat that I'd been around, but the one I wanted to pilot the most, the *USCG Cutter Eastwind,* the ice breaker in Antarctica, had eluded me. No matter how hard I tried, the real *Captain* wouldn't let me drive the big cutter!

Throughout my time in the Coast Guard, I had never forgotten the services that I had attended with Charlotte and her family at the Methodist Church back in Savannah. The minister's voice was still clear in my head, and I believed that my real life's mission was still ahead.

A month before my time in the Coast Guard was completed I received an envelope in the mailbag. It was something that I had been waiting on for a long time. I opened it slowly, not sure what to expect, but as I read the enclosed letter, a smile spread across my face; I had been accepted for the fall semester at Houston Theological College. I was going to study to become a minister!

CHAPTER 48

USCG Station, Fort Pierce, Florida
October 17th, 2004

I WAS out fishing off of one of the boats when I heard the loudspeaker calling out my name for a phone call. I got calls all the time; most of them were from my congregation, an unusual group, to say the least, so I wasn't surprised to hear my name called. As the Reverend Don Buckley, I was the leader of a *church* up the road from the station. It was actually at Archie's, a beachside bar, where every Sunday morning about a hundred people, sometimes more on a cooler day, would gather to listen to my version of God's way. I preferred to be called *Captain Don*, since I still saw myself as a captain of boats, and not a guardian of souls. My followers didn't care what I wanted to be called; they seemed to love whatever I taught them every week. My *flock* came to me for advice and guidance whenever things got tough, and I'd help them through their crises. I did this for everybody and anybody who needed my help; it didn't matter to me or God if you came to the bar on Sunday or not.

I had left the Coast Guard many years before, gone

to a theological college in Texas, graduated cum laude, and was ordained as a licensed minister. I took my new-found vocation and found work on any boat that would have me; I offered my willingness to work, my love of the water, and most importantly, my ministerial skills to anyone who needed them. I worked on shrimpers in the Gulf, crabbers in Alaska, and netters off the West Coast, and I honed my talents for boat driving and ministering wherever I went. I was a very happy man.

When the United States decided to invade Iraq, I was called up to active duty with the Coast Guard. They were sending younger men over to the Persian Gulf, so they needed to bring back some men to assist in their efforts at home. I was so excited to be back in that I signed up for a 10 year hitch. I imagined that it couldn't get any better than this. At the end of my ten years, I had been stationed here in Fort Pierce. Although it was a beautiful place, with the Fort Pierce Inlet, the Indian River Lagoon, and the Atlantic Ocean within its boundaries, the city had been known for many years as a *rough town*. At one point in the late eighties, it had earned the title of the 'Deadliest City in America' for cities under a half million people, so the *troubled* moniker definitely fit the city of Fort Pierce. I was sure that this is where God wanted me to do his work.

I had gone to the Station Commander to discuss my pending decision to either re-enlist or retire. I carried the rank of Senior Chief Petty Officer at the time, and the Coast Guard had made me an offer to be a Ship's Chaplain on board one of their cutters, but I wasn't sure that I wanted to leave Fort Pierce. I thought that I might offer the Commander my own deal.

"Sir, I've thought about your offer for advancement if I should decide to re-enlist, but I've made up my mind that I want to stay here in this area. Here's my offer: If the Coast Guard assigns me to this station permanently, I'll re-up for another ten years. I'll continue as the Station Chaplain and Counselor, and I'll do whatever else they need me to do, but they've got to guarantee me a permanent placement here."

The Commandant, Commander Rick Perry, and I had become close friends, and we were quite often found out on the docks at night fishing for snook and talking sports, especially Boston sports. Rick's passion for the Red Sox was almost equal to mine, and we never ran out of things to debate as we fished late into the night. He totally understood what I was looking for, and he agreed that he would try to secure the deal for me as soon as possible; he'd let me know the answer when he heard back from Miami.

The Coast Guard, eager to keep me on board, agreed to the proposal, and I signed up for another ten years in Fort Pierce. I had seven left on the morning I got the call that would soon upset the applecart for me and several of my closest friends.

"Captain Don here."

"Captain, my name's Ray Eldridge, from Sebastian. Do you remember me from my cousin's funeral last year? My friend CJ and I talked to you for a long time about fishing up here at the Inlet, and you had said that you'd like to come up some time to drop a line. Does that ring a bell?"

"It does, Ray. Wasn't that your friend who was attacked and killed by a shark up there?"

"Well, he was killed by somethin', but it wasn't no shark!"

"What was it then Ray? That's what the news was saying; in fact, haven't there been some similar deaths up there recently?"

"Yes, sir, that's why I'm calling you. I think I know why these people have been killed, and I need some help. I've got to stop what's going on now!"

"Ray, why are you calling me? Shouldn't you be calling the police instead?"

"Reverend, I need a *Holy Man*, somebody close to God, because what's killing these men is something evil straight from Hell! I have to see you today!"

Okay, Ray, that's fine. Can you come down to the Coast Guard Station, or do I need to meet you someplace else?"

"Can you meet me out at the Inlet, near the rest rooms? I can be there in an hour, Captain."

That's fine; I'll be there. See you then."

An hour later I was at the Inlet Park; I probably looked like anybody else spending time at the Inlet fishing, or swimming at the nearby beach. I was sitting at one of the picnic tables at the far end of the park. I was off duty, so I had my usual outfit of fishing shorts, a Coastal Angler T-shirt, one of my favorites, flip-flops, of course, and my faded old Boston Red Sox hat.

I'd bought the hat six years before when I went to see the Sox play the Marlins in Miami. I had thought that I'd never get to see the Red Sox play live again when I fled

Boston, but Major League Baseball had come up with *Interleague Play*, when teams from the American League played against teams from the National League. I had gone to all three games, and the Sox had swept the Marlins! It had been a great weekend despite the oppressive heat of the stadium there. If ever anyone needed a domed stadium, certainly it should be in Miami, but the owners couldn't convince anyone to fund a new stadium, so they continued to play in the Dolphins football stadium.

I didn't care; I had gotten to see the Sox, and I had started getting used to the heat here in South Florida. Summer here was about eight months long, usually, so it was something you learned to live with. I was already looking forward to next summer, when the Sox would be in town for four games; that would be a blast! Rick and I had already begun figuring out ways to not be at the Station for those four days; I couldn't wait.

As I sat sipping on a bottle of cold water, I saw an old pickup truck enter the parking lot. It stopped by the rest rooms, and the driver was looking around. I recognized him; it was Ray Eldridge, from Sebastian, and I got up and waved to the man. Ray pulled his truck up into a spot near the picnic table, and got out. As he walked over to the table, I thought that the man looked like *walking Death*, as my mother used to say.

"Hey, Ray, how are you?"

"Not so good, Captain, not so good" he repeated, as he shook hands with me. "Like I said in my phone call, I need help, and you were the only person I could think of who could help me with this bucket of shit! Oh, sorry, Captain, that just slipped out."

I just laughed out loud at that one; if this man had any idea how many times I'd used that word and countless other inappropriate phrases in my lifetime, he might not be able to contain himself. My former life on the streets of Boston, and my many years on boats, had taught me that men say what men say, and God sorts it all out. That's the way it was.

"Ray, don't worry about that. Sit down and let's hear what it is that's got you so knotted up."

"Captain, what I'm about to tell you is the truth, as I know it, but it's the craziest shit I ever come up with in my life. You'll understand when you hear my story."

Ray Eldridge told me everything that he had seen and done. He told me about the Golden Snake, and how big it was. He told me about the Park Ranger and his boy, and how they'd ended up just like the other men. Then he told me how he felt when he was knocked into the water with Eric.

"There was something powerful in the water with us; I couldn't see it, but I could feel it. It was overpowering, and it almost froze me, but I was able to get out of the water and back into the boat. That's when I took off, and never looked back! Whatever was in the water that day was evil, something straight from Hell, maybe the Devil himself, and we gotta stop it!"

"Whoa, Ray, let's slow down. The authorities have been reporting that it's a shark or a gator that's responsible for these deaths. That's a perfectly good theory, since we have both of them in abundance here in Florida. What makes you think it isn't one of them doing this?"

"Captain, I grew up in Sebastian. I've seen more

gators and sharks in my life as I've seen anything else. There's no way a shark, or a gator, that big, big enough to do what it's done, could get away from my boat without me seeing it. It just couldn't happen! This thing just disappeared as fast as it showed up, and I'm telling you that whatever it is in the water there, it ain't a shark or a gator; it's a Demon, guarding that gold snake, and we need to send it back to Hell!"

"Well, Ray, I don't know that we can say this is a demon or anything else from Hell, but this is what I'll do. I'll call a friend of mine who used to be in the Coast Guard like me. He's a History professor at Florida Atlantic University now, but his specialty is *Underwater Archaeology*. He knows all about the treasures along the beaches here; I'll ask him if there's any kind of record of a Golden Snake, or anything like it, from any of the wrecks that he's aware of. I've got another old friend who was stationed with me here that worked on a salvage crew up in Sebastian. She's a tour guide now at the Treasure Museum out on the beach, and she knows just about everything there is to know about the Spanish Treasure ships that have sunk off of the coast up your way. Those are a couple of good places to start; why don't you go home, and I'll give you a call after I fill them in on what's going on? I'm sure that we can trust them. And I know that they'll help us with whatever we need."

CHAPTER 49

USCG Station, Fort Pierce
October 22nd, 2004

My office phone rang; I was on duty, and had been counseling one of the sailors who had just learned that his brother had been killed in Afghanistan. The United States military was back over there again, trying to find the terrorists responsible for the attacks on the World Trade Center and the Pentagon in September of 2001, and it was not going as well as they hoped.

President Bush, like his father before him, had decided that it was the right thing to do, and had attacked Iraq again. He already had soldiers committed in Afghanistan, trying to ferret out the Al-Qaeda leader and his generals. Going into Iraq only stretched the military out, but everyone was sure that the Iraqi leader, Saddam Hussein, had been stockpiling weapons of mass destruction, or *WMD's*, as they were being called. While thousands of troops scoured Baghdad and the other major cities in Iraq, men like this man's brother were being killed almost every day in a country that the average American knew nothing about.

The Petty Officer had just left my office; it had been a tough couple of hours for both of us. I wanted to call it a day and head down to the dock. Taking one of the high powered boats out to sea and letting it rip was one of the most relaxing things I could think of; nothing made me feel better than blowing the quad 200's out until I felt like I was flying across the water. It was a great feeling!

The phone kept ringing.

"Captain Don Buckley" I answered.

"Hey, Reverend! How you doing? It's Pete."

Pete Harris was one of my closest friends. He had been calling me *Reverend* ever since he found out years ago that I preferred to be called 'Captain'. It was his way of busting my chops, and I'd gotten used to it over the years. Pete was a guitar playing, folk singer, who joined me at the bar/church every once in a while. He liked to tell people that his music was why they came out; it wasn't *my preaching*.

We had met when I first came to Fort Pierce. Pete was a local guy who, like me, had joined the Coast Guard years before, and then gone on to college after getting out. He had grown up hearing the stories and legends of the Treasure Coast, and took a special interest in the *1715 Spanish Plate Fleet*. His interests led him to a Master's Degree in History, and a Doctorate in Marine Archaeology; he was now a tenured professor at *Florida Atlantic University*, in Boca Raton, south of Fort Pierce.

Pete had come to the Station one day to do some fishing off the docks; I was already out there, and we struck up a conversation about fishing. After a few hours, I had asked Pete to join me for a couple of beers and a sandwich across the bridge at one of my favorite waterfront spots. We became good friends, and had spent countless hours fishing together ever since. He had joined Rick and I in the pursuit of fresh snook many times since our first encounter.

I had called him to discuss my meeting with Ray Eldridge. I had told my friend everything, not holding anything back. I described the haunted look in Ray's eyes, and the fear that still gripped him after his encounter in Sebastian. I described the golden snake just the way that Ray had, and I asked Pete to see if there was any possibility that this treasure had come from the 1715 Fleet, or any other wreck in the Sebastian area.

"Hey, Petey, what's going on with you?"

"Well, I've got some answers for you. It seems there might be some truth to the golden snake story after all. I spent hours in the library yesterday researching the manifests of all of the ships in the Plate Fleet. I've done it before, so I basically knew what to look for. Of all of the ships that crashed, there's been nothing recovered, or at least nothing that can be proven, from one of the bigger galleons in the group. It was a ship called the *Nuestra Senora de la Concepcion*, and there was no record of where it actually went down. Treasure salvagers have believed for years that it's the last great discovery, but nobody has found any proof of its existence."

"OK, but what's this got to do with the snake?"

"Hey, don't you preachers teach patience? I found the manifest for the Concepcion, and it wasn't quite the same as all of the other ships. It was carrying a large cache of Indian artifacts, mostly gold and silver, that was discovered in one of the old Mayan holy cities, Chichen Itza. Some of the pieces listed sound pretty incredible, but the clincher is this; they listed a six foot long, heavy gold chain, with the golden head of a serpent, as part of the inventory. I believe that your friend has found the first piece of treasure recovered from the *Concepcion*."

"So, his story has credibility, at least."

"Oh, that it does, Don, but that's not all that I learned. I did some digging in the archives, and found more information on the *Concepcion*, and its cargo. The snake was only one of many items that a group of Spaniards had found at the bottom of a Mayan sacrificial well. It's believed that all of the items found there were offerings made at human sacrifices performed by the priests, and that they had sent the treasures with the sacrificed people to the bottom of the well. You see, the Mayans believed that only the Priests and the Anointed Ones, the ones who were sacrificed, went to their version of Heaven."

"When the Spaniards found the snake, it is written that they lost all four of the men who found it to a 'serpent from Hell' before they were able to get out of the water. The relic was taken from there, and shipped to Spain for King Phillip with the rest of the sacrificial loot. While the Mayan treasure was on the ship in Havana, awaiting departure, several other men who were guarding it lost their lives. Two of the soldiers who died on the ship were found with their chests ripped open, and their hearts were missing. Sound familiar?"

"Oh my God!" My stomach had just done a flip; the idea that something like this could happen identically after almost three hundred years was more than I could rationalize. "How the hell could this happen, Pete?"

"You're the preacher. You tell me."

"You're right. I should never question the unthinkable; there's something going on here that could in fact be an evil force, like Ray claims. Good and evil have battled for supremacy throughout our history, and this thing is certainly a *black force*. Ray was right, Pete. There's a hell of a lot more going on here than a rogue shark; we've got to help him!"

CHAPTER 50

The Sebastian Inlet Treasure Museum, the same day

"Good afternoon, Sue Morgan speaking."

"Sue, it's Don, down here in Fort Pierce. How are you?"

"Hey, Don, I'm great! Couldn't be better, unless I was diving on a wreck someplace. What's up with you?"

"Well, I may need your help on something that may involve some of your expertise. Do you have a few minutes to listen?"

"Sure, Don, go ahead; I've got some time. It's been a very slow week around here, so there's not much to keep me busy."

He told her everything; he tried not to omit anything, because she could eventually play a valuable part in the mission. She let him go on without a single interruption, amazed by the story he was telling her. When he finally finished, he waited to see if she was going to be part of his team. It didn't take long to get the answer.

"My God, Don, that's an incredible story! I've seen

the reports in the local paper up here, and it's even made the news on some of the Orlando TV stations, but if it wasn't you telling it, I would have hung up already. Do you have any idea what this thing is, and do you have a plan that can work?"

"I have the beginning of a plan, but I'd like everybody involved to agree to whatever it is we decide to do. Do you remember my buddy Pete Harris, from the Station? He's coming up in the morning to meet me for breakfast at the *Southern Girl Restaurant* on Main St., in Sebastian. Can you meet us there? Ray will be there, too. It's up to the four of us to come up with something that can work."

"I'll be there; what time?"

"Nine AM. We'll see you then."

After hanging up the phone, Sue's mind went back in time to the early 'Nineties, when she had first met Captain Don Buckley. They had both been called up to active duty, due to the '*Gulf Conflict*' in the Middle East, and had been stationed in Fort Pierce. She had just lost her Mom to cancer, and was struggling to get through the days.

Captain Don had counseled her for several weeks, and a deep sense of gratitude had grown into a very strong attraction to the man who was helping her regain her life. Don Buckley was one of those people whose charisma seemed impossible to resist, and they were fast becoming good friends.

Knowing that he probably would never take the initiative, she had boldly asked him to go out to dinner and a movie, and she told him that it was on her. She actually was surprised when he not only agreed, but seemed to jump on the invitation with hardly a thought. Their first date went well, without a hitch, and he had given her a hug and a light kiss on her cheek at the end of the night. She was hooked!

They continued to see each other as often as they could, and the infatuation grew into something deep and meaningful for both of them. Things had started slowly with their dating over the first month, but taking the initiative again, she had asked him to spend a weekend with her at a nice beachside hotel in Fort Lauderdale.

She fell in love with Don that weekend. They had made love for the first time on Friday night, and they continued to share themselves with each other throughout the two days that they spent together. She couldn't imagine what it would be like to not have Don Buckley in her life.

They kept sneaking off to be together whenever they could; Don arranged his schedule with her duty times to maximize their time together. He had a friend, Steve Wild, who owned a picturesque Bed & Breakfast inn on the water in Sebastian, far enough away from the station to be comfortable. They would make the short drive up there and spend a night or two, but never let on to anyone that they were involved. Things were going very well for them until Don dropped a bomb on her one night.

"I was called into the Commandant's office this morning" he told her. "He told me that we were the talk of the station, and that as the Chaplain and counselor to everyone here, that I had put myself in a bad position. He doesn't feel that it's appropriate that I have a lover on base, and that it was very poor judgment on my part to get involved with you. He left no room for us to continue under these circumstances; he told me that if I wanted to be with you that I would have to resign my position, and leave the Coast Guard. I'm not ready to do that yet; my work here, and at my church, is why I'm here in Fort Pierce. I believe that it is my calling to be here, and I have to honor my commitment to God and the people that I help and serve here. We have to stop seeing each other; it has to end, Sue. I'm sorry."

She lost the light of her life that night. Don had become the most important person in her life, and just like that, he was gone. She spent the remaining few months of her time at the station doing the best she could to avoid coming face to face with the 'Captain'.

When her time was up, she moved to Sebastian, and started diving for a living. She did the best she could to move on with her life without Don Buckley, but weeks turned into months, and months into years, and she knew that this man was the only man she wanted to be with. Hearing his voice after so long only made her more certain of her commitment to him. This was the first time that she had spoken to him in years, and it had hurt like hell!

"Tomorrow should be an interesting meeting," she thought.

CHAPTER 51

USCG Station, Fort Pierce
October 22nd, 2004

I LISTENED as the phone rang, wondering if Ray would even answer it. On the seventh ring, a familiar voice answered.

"Hey, this is Ray."

"Ray, hello, it's Captain Don. Are you doing okay up there?"

"Yeah, I'm pretty much alright with everything; been waiting to hear back from you, though, what's goin' on? Did you talk to your friends?"

"I just got off the phone with them; that's why I'm calling. Pete's going to come up to Sebastian with me for a few days to help us deal with this problem. My other friend, Sue Morgan, from the Treasure Museum, is coming over, too. We'd like to hook up with you first thing in the morning to go over everything that's happened. We're meeting at the *Southern Girl Restaurant* at 9; can you join us there? We have an initial plan we want to lay out, and then we'd like to go out to the site where you found the chain."

"Are you shittin' me, Captain? You guys want to go out there? There's already four bodies been found out there, and I've been lucky enough to escape that sumbitch in the water twice now; do y'all think I'm nuts, or something?"

"I understand how you must feel Ray, but we've got to locate this thing before we can do anything else. If you don't want to go, then we'll have to find it ourselves."

"Oh shit, man, I can't believe I'm saying this, but I'll go if I have to. It's just that I keep thinkin' that my sorry ass has probably run out of luck."

"We'll only need you on the first day to help us locate the chain; if you don't want to take part in what we're going to try, you can walk away. I'd certainly understand if you did."

"Okay, okay, that's fine. I'll meet you at the *Southern Girl* at nine o'clock. We'll have some breakfast and listen to your plan, and then I'll take you to the spot. My boat's tied up at Suzy's Tiki Bar near the boat ramp, so it won't take us long to get on the water."

"That's great, Ray! We'll see you then."

CHAPTER 52

Sebastian
October 23rd, 2004

R AY had shown up at the Southern Girl early. He was working on his third cup of coffee when Pete Harris and I came walking in. He got up, shook our hands, and called the waitress over. Sue Morgan, as pretty as ever, had been sitting at another table, and had come over to his table when we had come in. She had come to me immediately, and had hugged me for quite a long time.

I was embarrassed a bit by this, so I broke away, and introduced the woman to Ray. She knew Pete Harris; they exchanged a warm handshake after *the hug*. Ray said hello to her and Pete, and we all settled in for coffee and a horror story.

We ordered some breakfast and started talking about our upcoming adventure. Ray spent about ten minutes telling them everything that he had done and seen out at the Inlet, and wrapped up his narrative by telling us that today just might be his last day here on Earth, so he might as well have a good breakfast. With that he launched into his omelet and home fries, letting me take over.

"Thanks, Ray! I appreciate you filling everybody in. As you might have guessed by now, I have a plan that I hope will work. If we recover the chain, we can decide what to do with it then."

"Oh God, Captain, I don't want no part of that friggin' shit-rope of gold! I want to be as far away from that damned thing as I can be!"

"No problem, Ray. I wasn't talking about keeping it, or selling it; I was talking about getting rid of it forever!"

"Okay, then! That's what I think we need to do with it, for sure."

Pete and I had decided on the drive up that we wouldn't tell Ray all that we had discovered. We felt that opening up the ugly history of the golden chain would only spook Ray out of cooperating with us, so we only told him what the plan for today was. Keep it simple, we had settled on; one day at a time. Sue, of course, had been told of the plan, and respected the call to not tell Ray everything.

"One day at a time", she mused, "the way it was for me when Don had shattered my world."

We finished up our breakfast, and headed over to Suzy's Tiki on the riverfront. We parked our trucks, and headed down the dock. It was a beautiful morning, with barely a whisper of a breeze. The water was almost like glass, and finger mullet schools were swirling around everywhere. Big roe mullet jumped out of the water and left big circles radiating on the surface. We jumped into the skiff, and Ray cranked it up. As it roared to life, I grabbed the lines and untied them. Ray turned the boat northeast, toward the Inlet; he sure as hell wasn't happy about this, but he knew that it had to be done.

"We have to find and destroy that damned golden snake!" Ray thought as he motored on out past the spoil islands. "That friggin' thing killed my best friend and three other guys, and I want to send it back to Hell where it belongs!"

He continued toward the South Park, and then veered off of the main channel, heading towards the area where he had originally seen the chain. He remembered everything about this spot; he'd already lost two men he had brought here, and he could never forget this location. He had driven his boat to it in countless nightmares, and it had never ended well. A few minutes after veering south, he slowed the boat.

"This is right about where I found it. I remember the markings on shore, and it was about twenty yards from that submerged tree over there. It's gotta be around here somewhere. When I came out here the second time with the diver, Eric, we had to loop around a few times before we found it. I'll start going in small circles, and you guys keep your eyes on the bottom."

Ray began moving the boat around in tight circles like he had talked about. As the circles became bigger, and farther away, from the original resting place, he started to think that they were getting too far away. He threw it into neutral and let the boat come to a slow stop.

"You know, I think we missed it. We're way too far away from the spot; we need to start over."

As we had been slowly circling, Pete had been thinking that maybe the Ranger and his son had managed to move it before they were killed. If that had happened, the area they needed to be searching was much larger than this section of grass beds. As Ray began slowing the boat, and had finished talking, Pete asked, "What if the Ranger got the chain out of the original location? What if he had found a way to get it out of there before his *accident?* We need to re-think our search, and expand the playing field. That's going to open up a lot of bottom; do any of you have any ideas about this?"

"I think that you could be right, Pete. Their boat was found around the other side of the park, in the main channel, drifting in an outgoing tide. The tide was about three hours out, so it would make sense that they were still on this side of the park when it happened, because the tide would have slowly been sucking the boat out into the South Channel. We could mark off a triangular area, starting at the first spot, and expanding it into a cone, starting just off the beach at the park, and going out about thirty yards to the south. That gives us a cone of about two hundred yards long to search, but I'm willing to bet it's in there someplace. They would have to have been in that area, since the sandbar to the left would have prohibited them from going too far in that direction. I think that we should go up to the beach, and start making back and forth swings, heading back to where we started. What do you guys think about that?"

"I say we try it. It's a lot of water to cover, but you're probably right. We can assume that it's somewhere inside this cone, so let's get started."

Ray put the boat in gear, and drove slowly to the point, just off the tip of the South Park beach. He turned the boat south, and started a slow troll across the channel area. On their fifth turn, Pete told Ray to stop the boat.

"I think I saw something *shiny* on the bottom. It was just a quick glimmer, but I know I saw something. Can you back up a bit?"

As we started to reverse, I said that I thought I saw something, too. Again, Ray cut the engine, and let the boat drift. Peering over the side, he was the first one to see the 'shiny' thing on the bottom. It wasn't the gold chain; it was an offshore fishing rod and reel, lying in about five feet of water.

"Hey, I see what y'all are talking about, but it ain't no golden snake. It's a heavy duty fishing rig for offshore. Some unlucky bastard must've lost it off his boat over the weekend. I'll get my gaff, and I'll pull it in; maybe it's got a name on it. Lot of guys get their names inscribed on their expensive rods, it's a status thing. Hold on!"

Pete had grabbed the gaff and handed it off to Ray. The gaff wasn't long enough; he was about two feet short of reaching the rod. "No problemo! I can fix that; can one of you get me my Duck tape, in my tackle box there? I'll tape the gaff to one of my rods, and then I'll be able to get it."

After the makeshift taping job was done, Ray once again dipped the gaff down into the water. This time he was able to get a grab on the rod and reel, and he slowly brought it up. It appeared to be a nice combo; a six and a half foot trolling rod, with a fairly new *Shimano TLD25* on it. The odd thing was that there was a length of line out on the reel that must have been about fifty feet. It was dangling in the water as Ray pulled his prize into the boat; he reeled it back in. "Sweet rig!" he exclaimed as it came up over the side, "I'm not a bluewater guy, but I can tell you that outfit cost somebody a few hundred bucks. It's a custom wrap; it hasn't got a name on it, but it has a number. We can call the rod builder in Stuart; it's a Crowder Custom, and they probably know who it belongs to."

Pete picked up his cell phone and dialed 411; a mechanical voice came onto the line asking him "What City and State?" God, he hated those damned computer answering services that all of the big companies used now; you had to repeat yourself five times, and then the voice would pleasantly tell you that it was sorry, no listing was found, blah, blah, blah.

"Stuart, Florida," he answered.

"What listing?"

"Crowder Rods, on Industrial Boulevard."

"I'm sorry, was that Chowder Roads, on Industrial Boulevard?"

"No, it was Crowder Rods!"

"The number is 772-678-4321", and we can connect you directly at no additional charge."

A voice on the other end of the line answered. Pete told him about a rod that he and his friends had just pulled out of the water in Sebastian. He told him how they'd like to return it to the unlucky fisherman who lost it, and could he tell them what the guy's name was? The voice told him to hold on for a minute after Pete gave him the number of the custom rod.

"Hello. Yeah, we built that rod for a Park Ranger at the Sebastian Inlet Park. His wife had it made for him for his birthday a few months ago; his name is Mark Thomas, and he lives in Floridana Beach on Sandpiper Lane, number 252. I've got his phone number, too."

"Uh, no, that won't be necessary. Mark Thomas is dead; he died in a horrible accident at the Inlet here last week. We'll turn the rod and reel over to the police. Thanks for your help."

They'd all been listening to the call, and they were standing with their mouths open, staring at Pete. Sue was the first one to speak.

"This rod belonged to Mark Thomas? Oh God, this is how he probably got that thing off the bottom. He must have hooked onto it, and tried to get away. This must be as far as he got; the chain must be somewhere between here and the place you found it before. We're on the right track, and Pete, you hit it on the head with your idea. Our cone just got a lot smaller, guys. Let's find this cursed piece of shit!"

Ray started the boat up again. The sputter of the engine was all you could hear; the four of us were silent as the boat wound its way back and forth between the beach and the sandbar. As we were slowly crossing back on one of our turns, Ray saw something that he didn't like at all. His heart almost stopped as he saw a large 'V' coming towards them in the water. "Holy shit, that friggin' things comin' for us! Look, it's heading our way over there!"

We all stood motionless, afraid to move a muscle. Suddenly a large snout broke the surface of the water about ten yards away.

"Damn! Can you believe that's a friggin' manatee? That thing just scared the livin' shit out of this old country boy! And I've seen a million of the damned things, too. I guess I'm a little strung out bein' out here. Shit, let's get back to finding that damned snake!" Ray said, as he tried to regain his composure.

Pete laughed a nervous laugh, and said that would be a good idea. With that, we started our hunt back up. About an hour later, I spotted it at the bottom; there was no mistaking this thing for anything but the golden snake. I was looking directly into the eyes of the serpent, since the head was facing up towards the surface, and I got a chill through my body like nothing I'd ever experienced. I began to silently mutter a prayer, because I knew that what lay below us was something very evil, something that God might not be able to help us with.

I told them that it was on my side of the boat, and asked Ray to bring over the crab trap we had told him to bring along. I dropped the trap onto the snake, and marked the spot with a trap float. Ray had traps all over the flats out here, and everybody knew that the lime green floats were his, so they were fairly certain that nobody would bother this trap.

"This is enough for today. Let's get back to town; we'll come back for this thing tomorrow when we're better prepared."

"Captain, don't you think you're leaving out part of the story here? How the hell are you gonna come back to get this thing?"

"That's tomorrow's surprise, Ray. Meet us at the North Ramp in the morning around nine. You'll see what's up our sleeves then."

CHAPTER 53

Sebastian City Boat Ramp
October 24th, 2004

"**G**OOD morning Ray!" I yelled out. "How's it going today?"

"I guess I'm okay, Captain. How y'all doing?"

"I'm feeling pretty lucky, Ray. We're going to get this damned thing today, I can sense it!"

"Well, I hope you're right. What's that thing Pete's got tied up to the boat?"

"It's a one man submarine. Pete borrowed it from the *Harbor Branch Oceanographic Institute* down in Fort Pierce. They use it for research and salvage ops, things like that. The University has a partnership program with the Institute, and they allow Pete to use it sometimes for his discoveries. He went down and got it last night. That's how we're going to get this thing, Ray. Pete's going to grab it, and take it out of the Inlet, as deep as he can go. Once he's out there, he's going to drop it to the sea floor, and let it rot there forever. What do you think; does that make sense to you?"

"Hell yeah, hot shit, what a great idea! I don't suppose he'll have to worry about that snake, or anything else, locked in that steel hot dog!"

"Well, that's what we think, too. Pete wants us to haul him and the mini sub out there and drop him off. He wants us to clear out, then meet him at the dock at the Inlet Park. He thinks it will take about three hours to get the chain and drive it out ten miles, then come back. He said the little sub can go pretty fast, so it shouldn't be hard to get this done in that time. We're ready to go; how about you?"

"I'm so ready I could scream, Captain! Let's go!"

Ray pulled his boat away from the ramp; it was a pretty quiet morning, and there wasn't anybody hanging around at the ramp. The South Ramp is where Sebastian's *social butterflies* would go to bitch and moan about everything wrong in town, but this facility was the less busy, especially during the week. He headed for the Inlet, confident that Pete's idea was going to rid them of that friggin' snake.

As he had the day before, Ray turned off to the right of the park, and slowly headed over towards the lime green float they'd left standing guard over their *treasure*. Ray stopped the skiff about twenty-five yards short; Pete had indicated that he wanted to get into the sub before they got there. He climbed over the transom, and walked up to the hatch on the sub. Opening it, he climbed down, telling us that he'd see us later.

"I'm going to take care of this evil bastard, Ray, I promise you. We'll never have to worry about it again."

He got in and closed the hatch. We watched as we heard the engine start up, and saw the single prop start to kick up bubbles. "Let's get out of here, Ray, it's in Pete's hands now. We'll see him soon enough."

"Okay, I'm good with getting the hell away from here. Let's go!" Ray turned the boat back to Sebastian thinking that it might be a good time to have an early beer at Suzy's. Yeah, that sounded good.

Pete came up on the crab trap rather quickly. Everything seemed to be the same as we had left it; he saw the glitter of the golden chain resting under the trap. The first order of business was to get the trap off and then grab the chain itself. He didn't expect these tasks to be too difficult, since the sub was equipped with a robotic *arm*. The arm was operated from inside, and it was so sensitive that the guys at the Institute said that it could pick up a dime from the ocean floor if you needed it to.

"Let's make this happen," he thought to himself. He started the arm moving towards the crab trap. He picked up the trap and moved it a couple of feet away, then turned back to get the chain. The clamps on the end of the robotic arm tightened down on the snake, and he started moving off.

As he watched in front of him, he thought he saw a blur coming from the arm. Suddenly, the little boat was hit by something powerful; it knocked the boat off course a bit, and Pete tensed. Picking up speed, trying to get out of there as fast as he could, Pete felt another slam on the side of his sub. The next thing he saw was something straight out of a horror movie; there, in front of his boat, was the fiercest looking snake he had ever seen.

The apparition was staring right at him; its eyes were like a molten volcano, set in the middle of a very large golden head. Its mouth was open, baring fangs that could rip a man apart with just a little effort. Taking it all in, Pete noticed something that was even wilder; the snake thrashing in front of him was being restrained by the clamplike jaws of the *arm*.

"Holy shit, Mother of God, what the fuck?" Pete thought. "That chain just came alive! This thing really is an evil monster, a real piece of Hell, and I've got to get it out of here!"

He kept the sub heading north, towards the tip of the South Park. The serpent kept slamming the side of the boat with its tail; each time it did, it knocked him around a bit, but he was able to stay on course. He didn't notice that each time the snake powered itself back and forth that the arm seemed to be loosening up from the hull. He turned the corner, and entered the South Channel. He headed east toward the mouth of the inlet; the water had gotten deeper, so he had taken the boat down a few feet. He felt another jolt slam the side of the tiny sub, and as he was trying to correct his course, he looked up to find the eyes of the serpent right in front of him, up against the glass nose of the boat.

"Oh shit! That damned thing is loose!" he said out loud, as he saw the arm of the sub still clamped on to the snake's midsection. The snake was swimming right in front of him, no longer attached to the sub. It was on its own, and it was seriously pissed off. Then he noticed some water dribbling into the boat, where the snake had pulled out the arm; it was collecting on the floor rather quickly, making him pretty uncomfortable as he thought about what could happen.

He had to get out of there; maybe make it to the beach, and see if the snake would follow him. If it didn't, he could run up to the Ranger Station. The only problem with that idea was that the station had to be at least a hundred yards away from the beach; that was a lot of ground to cover.

As he was thinking about his options, the snake had swum away from the front of the boat. Not seeing it now, he started to relax. "Maybe this is going to be okay," he thought. "Maybe he's gone, and maybe I'll be able to walk away from all of this."

The power that hit the sub from the side wasn't anything like what had hit him before. Apparently, the snake had moved off to gather his strength, and it had hit him full force on the port side. The tiny boat was knocked sideways, and Pete had to struggle to get it righted. A second powerful crash hit him on the starboard side and had the same effect. It was now fairly obvious to Pete that the monster wasn't going anywhere until he got to him. Naked fear tore through him like he'd never experienced before; "this could be it", he thought as he tried to rein in the horror of the moment.

As Pete fought to straighten the vessel, the snake had swung up in front of the boat. He was coming straight at the bow, toward the glass windows in the bow. Pete was pretty sure that it couldn't break the glass; it wasn't actually glass, it was the most indestructible type of plexiglas that was available today. It supposedly could withstand almost anything, he remembered from the manual.

The serpent hit the window head on; the force of the hit completely knocked Pete off course, and sent him toward the bottom. Once again, Pete worked feverishly to straighten the boat up. As he was struggling, he noticed small cracks in the bow window. He knew that he could be running out of time; he needed to get out of the water, and onto land. He might have a chance there, but he knew that he didn't if he stayed in the water. He pushed the engine as hard as he could, and he started to gain some speed. He was heading toward the beach, and the water was getting shallower. He knew he was close, but still had a ways to go. The puddle on the floor was about four inches deep, too, so getting out of the sub was his only option. That's when he saw the snake coming at him at bullet speed.

The snake hit the bow glass again; the blow was harder than the first, and the *impenetrable* glass started cracking in a spider web pattern. Pete knew he only had seconds left; he began praying. The snake would have him soon; he knew it was over. It was right in front of the breaking glass, staring at him. In his fear, Pete thought that the damned thing looked like he was smiling. The glass gave way, and the golden serpent burst through what was left of it; the last thing Pete remembered was the fangs of that unholy demon ripping into him. The sub sank to the bottom and drifted into the deeper water, taking Pete Harris with it.

CHAPTER 54

Suzy's Tiki, Sebastian
October 24th, 2004

SUE and I had joined Ray in an early celebration after getting back to the waterfront bar. Ray felt a whole lot more at ease, and had convinced us to join him in hoisting a couple of cold beers while we passed the time waiting to rendezvous with Pete. Beer drinking was something I only did on special occasions, but I was thinking that today was a good time to have a couple. It wasn't just what Pete was doing; I was excited to be around Sue again. She had volunteered to help, even after everything that had happened years ago; she was a very special woman, I knew that. Even though we hadn't needed her diving talents yet, I just liked having her around. It felt right. I wasn't even sure that we would need her at all, but something made me call her, and I was happy to have her nearby. I prayed that nothing would happen to her or my friend Pete. They had become two of the most important people in my life, and it really felt good to be working with the two of them again.

Ray talked about Sebastian and the fishing in the

area. He and CJ had been fishing the waters around here since they were kids, and Ray had a ton of stories about their years fishing together, so he amused us with all sorts of *fish stories*. The one that we liked the best was a story about a trip where they had been skunked all day; in a last ditch effort, Ray had told CJ that he was going to try one more spot behind a spoil island down by the Wabasso Bridge. Motoring along through the grass flats, Ray felt something hit him pretty hard right in the butt. Turning around, he saw a fat pompano flopping around on the deck. He immediately threw it into the fishbox, thanking God for helping two *shit luck* fishermen find something to eat for later. Ray thought that it was God's way of providing; they grilled up the two fillets later that night, vowing to get to church more often. That never happened, but they did catch a lot of pompano over the years. "One out of two ain't bad, right?" he had joked when he finished the story.

Ray, obviously, was feeling much better. It seemed that a large weight had been lifted off of his shoulders, and he was ready to move back into the life he had known before the golden chain had turned his world upside down. I felt a little rush of anticipation, too, as the time to go back out to meet Pete was coming up fast.

"Well, Ray, are you ready to head back out to the park? It's noon now, so by the time we get out there Pete should be pulling in from the Inlet."

"Yeah, what the hell, let's go! I'd rather stay here and have a few more beers, but I guess we should finish this up before I party too much."

"If we get this ugly affair wrapped up, I'm sure Pete

will want to come back here and join us. We can all celebrate together" Sue added.

We jumped into the skiff, and took off for the Inlet Park. At the tip of the park, Ray veered to the left this time. The dock was on the north side, off the main channel, near the Ranger Station; I saw that the flag at the station was still at half mast for Mark Thomas, and mentioned it to Ray.

"You know, Captain, I hope it's for all the victims, not just him and his boy. The other two men deserve some respect, too, ya know?"

"Of course they do Ray, but the Rangers were all much closer to Mark Thomas than any of the others. It's only natural that they honor their man, but it's okay to believe it's for them all."

Ray just shook his head in acknowledgement; he pulled the boat up alongside of the dock, and I jumped out with the ropes. I tied off the boat, and gave Ray a hand getting out. There was no sign of Pete, so Ray headed off to the Men's Room, over by the boat ramp. I needed to relieve myself of the two beers, so I headed for the rest rooms, too. Sue stayed behind to watch for Pete. A few minutes went by before Ray came back, and I followed behind a couple minutes later.

When I got back, the three of us went over to a picnic table near the dock, and sat down. It was a gorgeous day, and sitting there watching the water flow by and the birds diving on bait pods seemed to be a nice option to pass the time. Ray started telling us stories of the Inlet from when his father was a kid.

According to his Dad, back in the Fifties, he and his

friends would come out here to camp out for a few days. They had to let the air out of their truck tires to make it out to the rocks, since there wasn't a passable road. They'd fish, and hunt for sea turtles and manatees. Back then, it was legal to kill either one, and they'd set up a big fire pit and cook the fish they caught; if they were fortunate enough to kill a turtle or a manatee, they'd roast the meat over an open fire. His dad had an old bumper sticker on his truck right up to when he died that read *Manatee, the Other White Meat.*

"Well, thank God they finally passed laws against the killing of sea turtles and manatees. The way it was going back then, we might not even have any around today" Sue replied after Ray settled down.

"Yeah, I suppose so, but them friggin' manatees are such a pain in the ass, with all the damned laws about goin' slow every place you go. I know guys that would love to shoot every one of those damned things!"

"Let's hope they don't. They're really harmless creatures, and the tourists love to see them swimming around. People that visit the Treasure Museum love to look for them here at the Inlet, and down in the Seaway in Fort Pierce; dolphins and manatees are big business for the Tourist Council. When the manatees come into the embayment in the winter, people will line up five deep sometimes just to watch them in the shallow water of the canal. They do have kind of a loveable face; how could somebody shoot one?"

"Just like a deer, Sue. Everybody thinks they're so cute, but they sure do taste good."

This time Don piped in, "We're definitely on different sides of the fence on this one, Ray. I never could shoot a deer, and can't imagine I'd ever want to shoot a manatee, or anything else, really. I never had the hunter/killer mentality when I was growing up, and I certainly don't have it now. You must have heard that story 'All God's Creatures' haven't you?"

"I guess so, Captain. At least you like to fish, so you ain't half bad after all."

The three of us laughed about this for a bit. I thought about how different he and I were; we came from very different worlds, but were sitting here together on this beautiful day as partners in what we hoped would be a successful effort. Ray had grown up a country boy, learning to hunt and fish as a young kid, and Jackie Burke had grown up on the mean streets of Boston, carrying a gun for my own safety. The fact that I had never even pulled my gun out back in my *bad boy* days always made me feel better. Ray had been using guns throughout his life, and found nothing wrong with killing an animal or two. It was pretty weird.

Almost two hours had passed as we sat at the table, everybody taking turns telling stories from their past. There was no sign of Pete, and we were starting to wonder why he hadn't shown up yet. I'd tried his cell phone several times, with no response. Pete had told me not to bother, since it was next to impossible to get a signal in the sub, but I was getting nervous about the time. Pete should have been back here by now. It was closing in on three, and Pete had assured us that he'd be back by one, at the latest.

Sue could sense how nervous I had been getting; she

knew that *action was better than inaction*, so she came up with an idea to help get things moving. "Ray, I think we should get in the boat, and follow the path that Pete would have taken when he went out of the Inlet. He had said that he was going to go straight out about ten miles, then dump the chain to the bottom. Maybe he had some mechanical issues out there, or something. Would you mind going out to see if we can find him?"

"If you think that might help, sure, but if he's underwater, we won't see him, and he won't see us. It's up to y'all, whatever you'd like to do is good with me."

"You're right. It's a pretty big pond out there. We probably wouldn't spot him if he's underwater, but I sure hate sitting here doing nothing. Can we just go out a few miles to see if he's floating around out there?"

"Let's do it! Come on, grab the lines, I'm bored to shit sittin' here, anyhow."

Ray pointed the skiff eastward, and headed under the bridge. It was an outgoing tide, and the rip was pretty strong, but Ray knew where to go, and we were soon out in the open ocean. The Monster Hole, off to the right, had a large number of surfers riding its swells, as usual. Don thought about the two surfers who had discovered the second body; it was right there, where they were all sitting up on their boards.

"How quickly people forget. It's only been a short time since Eric's corpse was found floating there, and now everybody's back there surfing. It doesn't take much time for people to move on, Ray. It will get easier for you, too, you'll see."

"I hope so, Captain. What happened to those people

is partly my fault, and I don't know if I'll ever get over it, but I sure hope that I do!"

Ray headed due east, away from the beach, doing about twenty miles per hour. The waves weren't bad, and his old boat had no problems cutting through the swells. We had settled into watching the water for signs of the sub. We didn't speak; we were all pretty anxious to find Pete, so we put all of our concentration on scoping the surface of the ocean. The one to two foot chop made things a little difficult, but we soon got used to the bobbing of the boat. I wasn't sure how far out we'd gone, but it was now five o'clock, and there had been no sighting of Pete or the sub.

"Ray, it's five o'clock, man. I think we should probably head back in. Maybe Pete's there waiting for us; I don't have a cell signal out here, so I can't call him. How far out are we?"

"We're at least ten miles offshore. You're right, we need to get back. I'll pick up the speed on the way back, and it won't take so long. Hold on, I'm gonna nail it!"

The tide had turned while we were out there, and Ray was able to make the old boat fly. Sue and I held on, as the salt spray hit us in the face. I loved that feeling; the combination of speed and the salt air had become my passion while in the Coast Guard, and the cold splashes of seawater made me feel alive. Within a short time we saw the beaches, and then the Inlet itself. We'd be going under the bridge in minutes.

Ray slowed the boat down as he approached the Inlet. Even though it was an incoming tide, there were still some things that were floating around from the storms.

The junk seemed to stack up around the ends of the jetties, and kept moving back in and out with the changing of every tide. Being careful was the smart thing to do, since he didn't want to damage his prop, or worse yet, tear up his lower unit. As he got inside, he picked up his speed a bit, and headed for the dock.

We stared ahead as we got closer; passing the Ranger Station, we saw no sign of Pete, or the sub. As we bumped up against the dock, I jumped out. I tied the boat to the pilings, and started running toward the station. I needed to know if the men there knew anything about my friend.

Seeing a man jumping out of his boat and running at them full blast caused both of the rangers in the house to come out onto the porch. Not sure what was happening, one of them put his hand on his gun, just in case this was something bad. I reached the stairs in front of them; I was breathing hard, but I couldn't waste time.

"Have either of you guys seen somebody with a mini submersible here this afternoon? You know, like they use for research diving."

"No sir," one of the men answered. "We'd a noticed one of them if it was here. Hell, we don't see something like that around here except about once a year for the *Inlet Cleanup*. The divers use one to pick up trash off the bottom; they borrow it from the Harbor Branch, down in Fort Pierce. You wouldn't believe how much crap they pull out of here every year. It's unbelievable!"

"That's the one I'm looking for; are you sure nobody's seen anything today?"

"Well, we haven't. I saw you guys sitting out at the picnic table for a couple hours earlier; there's a fisherman who showed up right after you left, and he's fishing about a hundred yards east of the dock. He would have seen something if there was anything like that around. Why don't you go ask him?"

"Thanks, I will. Here's my business card; if you see or hear anything about my friend, or the sub, can you call me, please?"

"Yessir, we will. Sorry we couldn't help you. Good luck!"

"Yeah, thanks! I think I may need some right now."

I ran up the dirt road until I saw the guy fishing. I asked him the same questions, but the fisherman had seen nothing out of the ordinary. He added that it had been a very quiet afternoon there, and that it didn't even seem like there were any fish in the deep water in front of him. It was pretty strange, he said, because he always caught fish in this spot; it was his *honey hole*, he confided.

Ray and Sue had come up the road to meet me; I filled them in on everything, and we headed back to the dock. It was after six, and the sky was darkening up. It would be completely dark in a short while, and we wouldn't be able to see anything. The three of us weren't fooling each other at that point; we knew in our hearts that Pete hadn't got the job done, and we needed to make some major decisions. We got into the boat, and Ray gunned it back toward Sebastian. None of us said a word.

CHAPTER 55

Back at Suzy's Tiki Bar

THE boat bumped up against the dock pilings; Ray waited, expecting me to jump out and tie him off, but I just couldn't move. I was sitting in the seat in front of the center console, where I had planted myself when we left the park, and I was not interested in getting out of that seat. I was in shock that my friend Pete was missing and probably dead out there someplace, and we didn't even have a chance to look for him. My legs wouldn't work; I was crushed.

Sue called out to me "Hey, Don, are you alright up there?"

Ray joined in, saying, "Yo, Captain, you okay, or what?"

"I guess that depends on what you call okay. I didn't have a heart attack, or anything, if that's what you mean, but I don't think I'll ever be the same again. That man out there in that sub was one of my closest friends, and now I have a much better understanding of how you feel about losing CJ. Whatever it is that's out there has got to be stopped, and we need to come up with something pretty damned quick. I don't want to get anybody else involved in this, either, but I don't know how we can do this alone. I'm going back to the station tonight, but we have to find Pete and the sub as soon as we can. We have an incoming tide in the morning, so we'll have clean water to search in. We'll never find him after the brown water starts pouring out of the Inlet on the outgoing, so time is critical. Can you both meet me here at 7 in the morning?"

"Absolutely! I agree that we should bring nobody else into this pile of shit, but we might need to; I don't have a clue what to do now." Ray was in deep, and he knew that he had to see this through. To be part of something so important was starting to change the way he looked at himself.

"Well, I've got something kicking around in my head; I'll drive back down to Fort Pierce, and try to refine the plan. It might be the last chance we have to get rid of this damned thing! Sue, I'm going to need you to bring your dive gear; are you still willing to do whatever it takes? And will you be alright with diving for a short time if we need you to?"

"Of course, Don; I signed on for this mission just like everybody else here. I'll be fine, and I'm ready to do whatever you need done."

"Great! Thanks, we're going to need everybody to make this work, and I'm hoping that God's on our side. If he's not, then things could get real ugly."

"Well, Captain, I hope that your plan works tomorrow, 'cause I don't have a damned thing in my head except getting rid of that shiny bastard out there!" Ray added.

"Then I'll see you both here in the morning. Pray if

you believe, and please don't tell anyone what happened today, because I don't want to bring the police, or anyone else into this just yet. Let's see if I can make it happen tomorrow. Good night!"

I walked off the dock, and passed the bar, where there was quite a crowd of *Happy Hour* regulars knocking down a few drinks. I went to my truck, pulled out of the parking lot, and headed for U.S. 1 just up the street. Fort Pierce was about thirty-five to forty minutes south, so I'd have some time before I got to the Coast Guard station to think about our next chance to get that golden son of a bitch. It was a very long drive home for me; the thought of my friend lying dead at the bottom somewhere, the fifth victim of this horrific nightmare, was the only thing that I could think about. We had to get that evil bastard tomorrow!

CHAPTER 56

The North Boat Ramp, Sebastian
October 25th, 2004

R AY was at the ramp when I pulled up. He confessed to staying at the bar to have a few beers, but he assured me that he had spoken to no one about what had happened, or about what we were going to do today. He understood what I had said last night; this was on us to fix. We didn't want to see anybody else get killed by that snake, so he hoped that I had something good to try. This could be the best thing he ever did in his life, or it could be the thing that ended his days here.

"Whatever happens," he said, "this is for my buddy, CJ, and everybody else that bastard's killed; let's go fuck him up!"

"Amen, brother, let's go find that damned thing!"

Sue was pulling into the parking lot as they were talking. She got out of her Jeep, unloaded her gear, and joined them at the dock.

"Morning, guys! Let's get this done" she said, as she threw her tank and gear into the bow, untying the lines as she got in.

Once again, Ray headed towards the Inlet Park. It was another beautiful day on the Treasure Coast, and the river was flat and glassy. Trout, snook, and redfish were pounding the finger mullet pods that seemed to be everywhere, and we found ourselves wishing that we were going to be spending the morning casting our lines, and not trying to find another corpse.

We decided to start the search at the crab trap; the float was still there, so it was pretty easy to find. Ray pulled the boat up over the trap, and began a very slow troll towards the tip of the South Park. Pete would have to have gone this way with the sub, because that's where the channel was. The water on either side would have been too shallow, so he followed the channel to the point, and then turned the skiff eastward along the shoreline. He thought that Pete would have gone a little deeper here to avoid detection, so he sputtered along in about fifteen feet of water.

I had been right about the water; it was clean and green, and visibility was right to the bottom. It was a couple hundred yards to the dock, and another hundred, or so, to the Ranger Station, so Ray held his course as we all searched the bottom for any sign of Pete or the sub. We had seen nothing so far, which confused us; if the snake had attacked the boat, we didn't think that Pete would have gotten this far.

The dock was within fifty feet, and still there was nothing. Just before we got to the Ranger Station, we spotted the little sub below us. Ray stopped the boat, and grabbed his anchor.

"No, wait!" I yelled out. "Don't drop that here; I

don't want to be right over the boat. That damned snake is probably right around here somewhere, assuming that Pete got the chain this far. Go back to the dock, and tie up there; we'll go in from the shore near the fish cleaning table."

"Okay, sounds good to me. I'll bring her around." He turned the boat, and headed back to the dock. As I tied the boat off, Sue was already putting on her dive gear.

"That's good! I'm ready," she said, and she walked over to the little sandy spot near the table. Her mind had wandered back to her last dive, and her stay in the hospital. The words of her doctor had come back to her so many times; she knew that she wasn't in shape to do this, but she was the only one here to get the job done. She could only hope that her fragile heart would hold up long enough to see this through. They had to get this "treasure" and destroy it before it killed again. It was on her now; time to complete the mission. "I'm going in. Keep everyone away from here, Ray. You know what this thing is capable of; I'll see what it looks like down there, and be back as soon as I can."

Sue stepped into the water and disappeared below the surface. Ray and I sat down at the same picnic table that we had camped out on yesterday, and prayed that she would come up alive. Ray still had no clue what was going on, but he trusted me to get this done, so we just sat and waited. He'd know soon enough what my plan was, I figured.

It wasn't very long before Sue got to the tiny submersible. The incoming tide was moving pretty fast, but it didn't slow her down too much; she was swimming on adrenaline, and probably could have swum to Africa that day if she had to. The bow of the boat was facing eastward, so she took a large swing around the boat to get a look at it from the other side. She had seen no sign of the snake, but she was taking every precaution to make this plan work. She didn't know what else they could do if this didn't work.

As she swam around to the east side of the sub and came up on the front, she froze. She couldn't believe what she was seeing! The golden snake was inside the sub, curled up on the bloated corpse of Pete Harris. Her heart broke, as she knew how special this man had been to me. He was on a very short list of people in my inner circle, and even though I knew this had happened to my friend, the thought of confirming Pete's death wasn't something she was not looking forward to.

There was no way to get Pete out of there without disturbing the demonic creature curled up in his lap. This would affect the plan, but there wasn't any choice; she had to *go on with the show*, and get this done.

She swam back up to shore. Ray and I were sitting at the picnic table as she emerged from the water. She took her mask and fins off, and came over and sat down. Slipping off her tank, she turned to tell us the news.

"Guys, you're not going to believe what I just saw down there! That damned chain is coiled up on Pete's body, and it appears that we'll not be able to move it. This is going to change our plans, for sure."

"Change what plans, Captain? What the hell are you plannin' to do; will you at least fill me in now?" Ray had become very impatient, wondering what was up my sleeve.

Instead of answering him, I got up and walked over to the dock. I stepped down into the boat, and pulled my cell phone out of my shirt pocket. I hit a button, and then said "Hello, Rick, it's Don. I'm going to need that help we talked about last night."

Sue and Ray could hear a voice on the other end of the line, but couldn't tell what was being said. "I'm going to need it ASAP, sir. We've got to go back in the water to hook up the chain. That shouldn't take too long. If we can get that done and get back up to the surface, we might be able to complete the task. Please hurry, Rick. I don't know how much time the Good Lord will give us for this job, but I'll be praying the whole time!"

I hung up the phone, and came back to the table. I sat down, and proceeded to tell Ray and Sue what we were about to do.

"I started thinking last night on the way back in that there had to be a way to get rid of this thing. Pete and I had thought his plan with the sub would work, but that certainly didn't end too well. And we had talked about the Park Ranger, and how he had probably tried to hook this thing, and then head away as fast as he could. Well, that didn't work, either, but I still think that the Ranger, and Pete and I, were on the right track. We have to get this chain, and its evil *watcher*, out of here, and drop it offshore as far away as possible. That's when I came up with this plan for today, and I just put it into motion. The U.S. Coast Guard is on the way."

"The Coast Guard! Captain, I know that y'all have some pretty fast machines down there, but how can they get away in a boat any better than anybody else has?"

"Well, that's the kicker right there, isn't it? We're not going to be doing this in a boat, Ray."

"What the hell are you gonna do, then?"

"Right now, Sue has to go back in; she's got some work to do."

I went over to the boat, and picked up a large steel chain that I threw into the water just west of where the sub was. I grabbed a shorter chain with a hook at the end, and walked toward the water. Ray had seen me load them, and figured that I planned to use them for pulling the sub up, but now he wasn't sure. Pete's body was still in the seat at the front of the sub, and Ray thought that I must have figured out how to get him out first. "How was he gonna do that if that *Golden Snake* was sittin' in the guy's lap?" he thought, as he watched me hand the steel chain to Sue. She instantly disappeared below the surface.

The added weight of the chain brought her to the bottom pretty quickly. The tide was getting slack, so she was able to swim towards the sub, dragging the chain just below her. She slowed up as she closed in on the boat. If she did anything to warn the *watcher,* she would be dead in seconds, and this plan would be done. She had to be smart; it was the only way she'd beat this bastard!

She was at the stern of the boat, and there was no sign of the monster. She walked herself along the port side of the sub, and put the hook through the steel loop on the top deck. That's how the research ship pulled the sub up from the water when they were at sea, so she knew that it would be strong enough to hold the weight. She let the hook down very slowly, making sure that she didn't make a sound. She gently walked away from the sub, holding the chain in her hand, letting it out as she moved away.

A blur of color went by her on her right side. She didn't see what it was, but she knew that something big, and very fast, had just swam past her, not very far away. She dropped down onto the sandy bottom, and lay as flat as she could, expecting the worst. Her eyes saw something coming towards her; it was a bull shark, about eight feet long, and it had been attracted by the movements she had been making. Bull sharks were a common occurrence around most of the inlets along the Florida coast, so she had run into them before. She knew that they could be very aggressive, so she needed to be completely still as the big shark swam up close. Taking a long look at the woman, the shark veered off, and swam away.

She started her bottom walking again, reaching the second length of chain that she had thrown into the water. She attached the two pieces of steel link together with a locking connector, and after making sure that the bond was solid, she swam back to shore. Ray and I had seen her bubbles, and came over to meet her.

"What's goin' on, Sue? I'm guessing you just hooked that chain up to the sub, but what about Pete? What are you gonna do about him?"

Ray was still confused by what was happening. I decided that it was time to bring him in 100%. "The original plan was to get Pete's body and the sub up out of the water. But now that we know he has company in there, we have to use it to our advantage. There's nothing we can do about Pete; he's going to have to stay in the sub. We can't chance losing this battle trying to rescue my dead friend; we're going to take the submersible out to sea and he's going with the chain, Ray, that's all we can do." I must have looked pretty cold at that point, because Ray looked at me like I was stone. His face told me what he was thinking. I assured him that there was no other way to do this, and too many lives, including ours, were involved to not get this job done.

"Holy sheee-it!" Ray Eldridge was blown away by my statement, but he certainly understood the predicament and the risk involved in trying to get Pete out of there. As he stood there with his mouth open, and his mind flying, they heard the loud roar of a large helicopter. It was then that Ray figured it out; the *Golden Boy* was going for a ride!

CHAPTER 57

Sebastian Inlet State Park, that same day

THEY looked up to see the large rescue chopper from the Coast Guard station. It was dropping down into the parking lot right next to them, so they covered their ears, and got out of the way. Ray could only see one man in the helicopter, the pilot, who sat the chopper down, and opened the door. Don ran up to him, and shook his hand.

"Rick, this is Ray Eldridge, the guy I told you about last night. And, I'm sure that you remember Sue. We're glad to see you, but I just want to give you one more chance to back out of this deal if you want to change your mind. "I have something important to tell you before we get started. Pete's body is still in the sub, and there's no way to get him out. The chain is wrapped around him, and I don't know of any way that we could get him out of there without bringing all Hell down on us. He's going to have to stay where he is; there's no alternative. Are you alright with that?"

"Does Pete have any family?"

"No, he doesn't. He's never been married, has no

kids, and his folks have been gone for quite a few years, as I remember him saying. Aside from the people he works with, I'm probably his closest friend."

"Well, I don't like it, but if there's nothing that we can do, then I guess that we should proceed with the mission. I wouldn't have just flown this bird up here if I didn't believe that what you're doing is the right thing. Five people are dead already because of this thing, and Pete was a friend of mine, too. So let's get it as far away from here as we can. Are you ready? As I said before, go ahead and hook us up."

"I am as ready as I can be; did you release the winch line on the bird?"

"It's loose. Hook it up to your chain, and we'll bring it up."

The Coast Guard station had two *search and rescue* choppers in Fort Pierce. Rick, as Commandant of the station, had this one fueled up first thing this morning, waiting for my call. He had cut his teeth on the rotary birds, training and flying on the older Sikorsky HH-3F Sea King, the original helo used for years by the Coast Guard and Navy both. This was the newer Sikorsky version, the HH-60J Jayhawk, and Rick loved to fly it whenever he had a chance. He had hung up his *wings* a few years ago as he advanced in rank, but had earlier flown hundreds of missions in the Coast Guard helicopters. This mission, I assured him, was not going to be like any other he had been part of.

Before I had a chance to engage the hook, the two Rangers came up to see what was going on with the helicopter. They always monitored Channel 16, listening for

Mayday calls, or trouble nearby, but they hadn't heard anything on the radio about a Coast Guard helicopter landing out in front of their station.

"Hey guys, what's going on? Has there been an accident? We haven't heard a thing on the radio."

Commander Rick Perry took control of the situation. "We've got a bit of a problem, Ranger. My friends here were doing some diving, and discovered something that might be a drum of toxic waste. We're hooked up to it, and we're going to pull it out. I think it might be a good idea if you clear the area around here just in case the drum bursts, or something. We'd certainly appreciate it if you could give us your assistance."

"Oh, hey, no problem, sir; there's just a couple of fishermen up the road towards the bridge, but we'll pick them up in the truck and take them over to the North Park."

"Thank you so much! That's great!"

The men waited as the two rangers jumped in their truck and headed away. As soon as they were out of sight, the Commander called out to me.

"As I was saying, why don't you hook us up, and we'll pull that damned sub up and take its nasty visitor for the ride of his life!"

I grabbed the winch line and connected it to the chain from the sub. I ran back to the helicopter; Sue was inside already, and while I was climbing in, Ray came over to board the bird, too.

"Ray, I'm sorry, but you can't come along for this ride. If something happens to us, you'd be the only one who knows the real story about all of this. If we're not successful, and we don't make it, go straight to the State Police, and tell them everything. Tell them they may need to nuke this bastard back into Hell, but make sure they understand how evil this thing is. We need you to get in your boat, and get the hell out of this area as soon as you can. Go, now, and we'll wait for a few minutes before we lift that sub out of the water. Hurry!"

As pissed off as he was about not going, Ray knew that I was right. If we didn't get this done, somebody had to know what was happening. He shook everybody's hand, and wished us luck.

I called out to him as he ran to his boat. "It's in God's hands now, Ray, but we need all the help we can get. Pray that we meet up later for a cold beer at Suzy's!"

Ray acknowledged me with a quick wave and jumped in the skiff, untying his lines as he did. He started the motor, and took off toward the North Park, on the other side of the Inlet. He wanted to make sure that he at least got to see that sub and the evil monster in it flying through the air below the helicopter. It might not be a front row seat, but at least he wouldn't miss the whole show. He was across before he knew it, and he steered his boat into the shallow cove between the jetties. He heard the blades of the big chopper revving up across the water.

As the Commander raised the bird slowly, I looked out of the open doorway. I was watching the chains, because I needed to let Rick know when they were beginning to straighten up. I told him that it was just about time, and he put a little power into the winch. As the bird began to lift the sub off the bottom, we heard some weird creaking noises, but the cable held. The sub broke the surface, and was suspended about ten feet over the water.

I looked into the small boat below him, and what I saw then was much different than what I'd seen so far. The golden chain in the sub had been replaced by a living thing of some sort, and it was staring at me, with its eyes boring into me like a saw cutting into flesh. I was as scared as I had ever been in my life. I thought back to that night long ago in Boston, at the Police Station, and how scared I thought I was then. I remembered the night I was shot in Savannah, and how much that had scared me, but nothing compared to this. This was a paralyzing fear, and my body seemed to tighten like it was being squeezed by a giant vise. I could feel my body shaking, but I had no control over it. "If this isn't the Devil himself, then I pray to God that I never get to meet him!" I thought.

"Don, are you alright? What's the matter?" Sue had never seen any man look as scared as I appeared to be, and that scared the hell out of her!

We had always assumed that there was something alive that was doing the killing, but we had never thought that the golden chain itself could actually be the monster. Pete and I had discussed this theory on the first night, and we concluded that there must be a guardian, or *watcher* of the chain that was always nearby to protect it. That had even sounded a little crazy, but it was the only answer that either one of us could come up with. Sue and I had made the same assumption; we thought that if we got the chain out of the water, and away from its *keeper*, then we would be free to take the cursed chain out to sea. Now we had been dealt a new set of cards, one that we could never have dreamed up. The chain had been wrapped in

Pete's lap, and now that they were in the air, there was something very alive staring up at him. "What the hell is going on?" he mumbled to himself.

"Guys, I know that this is going to sound crazy, but that chain down there seems to have come alive, and it's the most fearsome thing I've ever seen in my life. I don't know how to explain this, but I have to believe in Evil if I'm going to believe in God! This is how these men have been killed; this creature from Hell is what's tearing them apart!"

"Oh damn! Is it moving, or doing anything at all?"

"No, it's just staring up at me."

"Then I'm going to keep moving. Let me know immediately if something's happening."

As I pulled away from the window, Sue moved to see what it was that had frozen me to the spot a couple minutes before. Looking down at the sub, she immediately saw it with her own eyes. It was the most hideous thing that she had ever seen in her life, or in her nightmares, for that matter. She knew then that they couldn't fail; they had to get rid of this evil beast.

The Commander had decided to fly the chopper under the bridge, not wanting to take the chance of losing his cargo. He knew that he had just enough room, so he proceeded to pass beneath the moving cars above. Some of the cars had stopped up on the bridge, and the owners were standing there watching the big bird fly underneath them. They had no idea why he was flying a mini submarine below his helicopter, but they all thought it was great entertainment.

He was over the east end of the Inlet, with nothing

but thousands of miles of the Atlantic Ocean in front of him. The plan was to fly out past the Continental Shelf, and then drop the sub into the deep waters below. The *Melbourne Canyon* was about thirty-one hundred feet deep about fifty miles out, and that was their destination. So far, everything seemed to be going well.

Rick Perry had no idea of the terror running through his friends behind him. With the maneuvering of the bird under the bridge, and trying to make sure that he didn't lose the sub, his attention wasn't on the cargo hold. He turned around to tell me that it was clear sailing, but he saw that there was something definitely wrong.

"Hey Don, I was about to tell you that it should be less than an hour before we send this thing to the bottom. What's up? Is there a problem back there?"

"It appears that our friend down below is very upset, and it's watching everything that's going on. I'm nervous as hell that he's going to do something nasty before long."

"Well, it shouldn't be long before we're deep enough to drop him if we have to; I'll let him go as soon as there's a problem. I'd rather be in three thousand feet of water, but right now we're close to two hundred. Just let me know, and I'll pull the release."

"Okay, good enough." I peered out the open door to the sub below. The snake's golden head was closer to me; it appeared that it had raised itself up, as if to strike, and its body was half out of the sub. The eyes were burning fiercely, and once again, I felt the uncontrollable tightening of every muscle in my body. As I stared back at the creature it began to move; it was wrapping itself around the steel chain!

"Rick, the damned thing is climbing up the chain!" I screamed through the noise of the blades. "We need to do something now to get rid of this thing!"

"Oh shit! Are you kidding me? Close the door and strap in, people, we're going for a ride!"

As soon as the Commander saw that we were belted in to the jump seats, he hit the stick. The helicopter dipped sharply, making both of us feel like we just lost our stomachs. He turned the yoke hard to the left, and once again the chopper responded. A similar move to the right had the same effect. I looked down into the sub below me; the serpent was back inside the boat. Rick's tricks had worked for now. I let Rick know that everything was alright, and I told him to keep going.

Rick accelerated a bit, not wanting to lose the sub just yet. The area we were over was one of the best fishing grounds on the East Coast of Florida; there were hundreds of recreational fishermen and dozens of commercial boats that worked the waters below them for billfish, dolphin, kingfish, wahoo and great bottom catches like grouper and snapper. Releasing the snake here was a risk; the chances of somebody discovering it while fishing or diving were too high. We needed to continue with our original plan of a deepwater drop.

We flew on towards the Canyon. Minutes passed, and we began to relax a little. The snake was still in the sub, and hadn't made any further attempts to climb the chain. Rick made a navigational adjustment, and pointed the bird towards the southeast. That's where the deepest part of the Canyon was, and we all thought that the possibility of a discovery by anyone else out there was pretty remote.

We had all been talking for a few minutes when Sue got up to check things out. She peered down into the sub and saw nothing. The serpent wasn't there!

"Commander, the snake's not in the boat, and I don't see it! We may have lost it; it must have dropped out of the sub."

"Well, maybe it's for the best. We're in over four hundred feet now, so that's not so bad, and we've still got the sub, and Pete's body; now we can give him a proper burial."

I felt better for a moment; we had rid ourselves of the serpent, and now I'd be able to give my best friend a proper funeral. "I guess you're right, but I'd love to know for sure what happened. I don't want to ever have to worry about that thing killing again; this kind of leaves it hanging, if you'll pardon the pun."

We all chuckled lightly, and Rick started to turn the chopper around. As he banked to the left, we heard a noise outside the door of the cargo hold. Sue got up immediately and went to the door; opening it wasn't an option, so she held her ear up to it to see if there was anything she might hear.

Boom!

Sue jumped back away from the door; her heart was racing so fast she thought that it might burst! We hadn't lost the snake; it was still with us, and somehow it was right outside that door. Fear spread through us as it had never done before; we were in trouble, big trouble, and although we had won a couple of battles, we weren't sure now that we could win the war.

"How the hell is that damned thing holding on out there?" I yelled to nobody in particular.

"It's a damned big snake, Don. It's probably using its tail to secure itself; haven't you ever seen how snakes do that on branches of trees, or on posts? He's doing that to secure himself to the chopper, I'm sure, which only gives him so much room to stretch out. I'm going to have to try to dump him again. Strap in, it's party time!"

Rick made a sharp turn back toward the southeast; he wanted to get out as deep as he could again, and he was hoping that he could shake this thing off his chopper along the way.

Boom! The snake again hit the side of the door with a vengeance. We both thought that it seemed stronger and louder than the first time, which made us both a little more anxious. I had started praying after I slowed my heart down a bit, and I was mumbling every prayer I knew that was meant to thwart the Devil, because I was sure that this monster was certainly a servant of Satan himself.

Rick turned the yoke as hard as he could to the right, then to the left. He dipped sharply, and came up as vertical as he could.

Boom! Their guest was still with them; it had figured out a way to hold on, and was ready for the maneuvers this time.

"Have you got any other tricks up your sleeve, Rick? I don't seem to be getting the miracle that I'm praying for."

"I have only one thing left to try guys, and it may be the only thing that can work. We're going to have to blow this bird to Hell, and hope that it takes this bastard with it! Don, I need you to do some things. Get a lifejacket and helmet on, and find the emergency flare gun in the back. There's a tool kit back there, too. Find a screwdriver, and a hammer or something. Sue, you need to put a jacket and helmet on, too, and bring one up for me. I've got to call this in."

"Call what in? What's going on?"

"Like I said, Don, I'm going to blow the chopper out of the sky, and we're going to jump just before I do. We may all end up dead, but staying in this bird isn't the safest plan for longevity. I'm going to call the station, and have them send the other chopper and every boat that's available out to our GPS points when we jump. Get your jackets on, and get that stuff; we're coming up on the Canyon fast. We need to move!"

As dangerous as this seemed, I realized that it might be the only way to kill this golden monster, and, despite the chance that we might all get blown apart in the blast, I knew that it would be the right thing for us to do. I found the flare gun and a Phillips head screw driver and grabbed a large wrench, too. I brought the items up front to Rick.

Rick was on the radio, on a private channel. He had told the radio man to get the Lieutenant Commander on the radio as soon as he could, and he was waiting for him to get on. When his Junior Officer got on, he quickly told him that he had an emergency at sea, and that he needed him to dispatch every available man to the GPS coordinates he gave him. He explained that he had to blow the helicopter, and that he, Captain Don, and a woman named Sue Morgan were going in; speed was most important. As the Lt. Commander stammered a response, Rick told him that this was truly a *life or death* mission, and he needed to implement it now. He'd answer any questions later. He signed off, put the chopper on autopilot, and grabbed the screwdriver and wrench. He headed back into the rear deck.

We watched as he lifted the central panel in the floor. He opened it all the way, and then he climbed down into the belly of the helicopter. He found the fuel tank, put the screwdriver up next to it, and banged it through the tank with the wrench. Fuel started leaking onto the floor, forming a puddle around the tank. Rick climbed out and left the hatchway open.

They weren't positive about where the serpent was, but all of the noise it had been making had been coming from the right side; Rick made the decision.

"I'm going to throw the door open on the port side, and hope that our friend isn't staring us in the face; so far, he's been on the starboard side, so I think it's the right choice. When I open that door, the both of you jump out as fast as you can; I'll be right behind you. We're about a hundred feet over the water, so there's going to be a little jolt when we hit, but we should be fine. My men are on the way; as long as I kill this bastard in the blast, we'll be alright. If not, then I'll see you in *Sailor's Heaven*. Go, now!"

He threw open the door, and pushed Sue and I out. Aiming the flare gun, he shot it into the open doorway, and into the hatch. Then he jumped out, seconds behind Sue and I. He was about twenty-five feet from the water when the explosion knocked him into the ocean. He was knocked unconscious from the blast, and went under the water; his lifejacket did its job and lifted his head up into the air. He floated there for several minutes before I was able to grab his head and get him squared up. Sue was swimming towards us; we had all made it.

"Rick, I don't know how we survived that! Oh my God, I swear I thought that we'd all be dead, but here we are. But I can't help wondering whether or not we killed that damned thing. Did you see anything before you jumped?"

"Not a thing, Don, but we'll soon find out if we didn't, don't you think? You said he was pissed off before; well, he must be *nuclear* pissed off now!"

Sue reached them in time to hear that last comment from the Commander. All she could think about was that I was safe, and that we were going to be okay. She hadn't thought about the blast not killing the serpent.

We all laughed nervously; we knew that if the serpent had survived the explosion, we probably wouldn't be around for Rick's men to find us, so a little comic relief seemed good for our nerves. We floated there together, recounting the events, and everything that had just happened. As the minutes flew by, we started feeling that we had indeed completed our mission; there was no sign of our nasty enemy.

A noise in the distance caught our attention; it was a very powerful boat, and it was coming our way. As it closed in on us, we recognized it as the thirty-six foot power boat that we had confiscated from some drug runners a couple of years ago. With quad 200's on it, it was the fastest boat in our fleet, and now it sported the colors of the U.S. Coast Guard. It had always been my favorite boat, and now it was Rick's. We waited as it approached.

The big boat pulled up alongside of us a few minutes later. The men threw life rings out to us, and then pulled us all up into the boat. Cheers went up from everybody; it seemed that we had made it, and that the mission was indeed a success.

"Petty Officer, let's get this boat back to the station. I need to make some calls."

"Aye, aye, sir" the sailor replied, and revved up the motors.

I stood up and raised my hands, and asked the Petty Officer to stop the engines. I was Reverend Don Buckley, their Chaplain, and as every man on the boat went quiet, I began to speak.

"Gentlemen, today I lost a great friend and a hero, who played a tremendous role in what we just accomplished. Even though none of you know what's happened here today, I'd like to ask you to join me in a *Burial at Sea* for a fallen comrade and former Coast Guardsman. His name was Pete Harris, and he played a mean guitar!"

"Please join me now; The Lord is my shepherd, I shall not want...."

As the glitter of gold pieces fell from the sky and hit the waters of the Melbourne Canyon, hundreds of fish were attracted to the area. They had watched as large pieces of metal and debris had fallen, but it was the gold that had attracted them. They thought that it must be a big bait school, and, one by one, they tried gulping down the shiny gold fish.

They spit them out as soon as they felt the hard surface. The pieces weren't anything tasty, so they let them drift to the bottom, three thousand feet below. As the gold sank lower in the water column other fish were drawn to it, thinking the same thing as the surface fish. But they spit it out, too, and it all finally settled to the bottom with the rest of the debris. It would be swallowed up by the shifting sands of the bottom over time, and it would never be seen again.

There was one large piece that didn't disintegrate like the rest, though. It had settled into some rocks at the bottom. Its bright red eyes peered out over the ocean floor, seemingly watching everything in its sight. The shiny head of the snake, with the fiercely gleaming eyes, was enough to scare off any other bottom dweller; there wasn't a fish to be found within a mile of those rocks.

The Golden Serpent had found its eternal resting place. God help anyone who ever found it again!

EPILOGUE

Marsh Harbour, Abaco, Bahamas
November 6th, 2004

"WOULD you two like another Pina Colada?" asked the bartender. He was a British *ex-pat*, as he liked to be called. He had been in the Bahamas when England had still controlled them, but he had never gone back to London after the Bahamas became a sovereign nation, like he thought that he would. Life was just too damned good here!

"I think I would; how about you, Mrs. Buckley?"

"I can't think of another thing I'd rather be doing right now, unless you count going back to the house for a little playtime."

When Sue and I had gotten back to the station in Fort Pierce, and finally had a chance to be alone, I had told her that I never should have brought her into our circle, but that I was drawn to her, and that this had seemed like a good time to bring her back into my life. That was rather ironic, I had said, given that we all might have lost our lives that day, but being with her again had made me realize how much I had missed her over the years.

I told her that as we were all floating in the water waiting for the boat to arrive, that I couldn't remember a time when I was so happy to see somebody swimming towards me as I had been when I first saw her after the explosion. Knowing we had been successful in our mission and we were both alright made me understand that she was part of God's plan for me, also. I had proposed to her right there, in my office at the station, and she had accepted without blinking!

Our destruction of a U.S. Coast Guard helicopter and the tiny submersible helped me get an early retirement. I wished everyone well, and told them I'd be back someday; I just didn't know when. Sue resigned her job at the museum, and we left for Abaco in the Bahamas the next day. A local Merchant Captain out of Fort Pierce that I had worked with had a vacation spot over there, and after he pronounced us *Man and Wife*, he handed me the keys, and told us to stay as long as we'd like.

We both felt that it could be a very long time before we left these beautiful islands; we had found a place to be together, away from the craziness that we had just endured, and there was an opening for a minister at a church over in Hope Town, just across the water from Marsh Harbour. The job came with a small cottage and an old boat. Sue and I had visited the church two days ago, and had fallen in love with the quaint little island and its people. We had decided to accept the post and live out our days together in this wonderful corner of the world. I didn't think it could get any better for us, and we both felt that we deserved some peace after our battle with the Devil's serpent. Life here, after all of our trouble, would be good for us.

I was about to confirm the two Pina Coladas, but thought for a second about Sue's idea. We could always drink later. "You know, Alan, I think I'm going to skip that drink. Could you call us a cab, please?"

ABOUT THE AUTHOR

Mark T. Bradbury now claims the central east coast of Florida as his home for twenty years. Living on the Treasure Coast, named after the incredible gold and silver-laden Spanish galleons that crashed on the near-shore reefs in 1715, he's been reading and listening to the legends of the local treasure seekers since he arrived. His enthusiasm and exploration in Mayan culture, coupled with his fascination for treasure hunting, led to *Serpent's Curse*, a combination of the two interests. Visit mtbradbury1.blogspot.com to learn more!

TURN THIS PAGE AND GET A
GLIMPSE OF THE NEXT CURSE —

SERPENT'S RETURN

CHAPTER ONE

Fort Pierce, Florida
April 20, 2008

"Everybody in this room knows that until we get their attention nobody's gonna give a damn about what's going on here in our harbor. We've got the US Coast Guard Station right there on the Seaway, and they don't seem too interested in stopping what's happening."

"So, what are you proposing, Jack? What can us 'little guys' do that's going to stop the rampant pollution of our Lagoon and Inlet?"

"I'm just saying that we need to do something soon, Bob, or there won't be an edible fish, crab or clam anywhere near here. It's gotta stop, and it looks like we're the ones to do it. Nobody else is stepping up; we've got to get this fixed now!"

"Jack, we all know that the government and Big Sugar are letting this happen. It's just business as usual for our politicians. They hear us complain, come and visit, then go back to Washington and sit on their collective asses. Their payday is just around the corner at the next election; Big Sugar will pour millions of dollars into their campaign war chests, and absolutely nothing will be done to change anything in the Indian River Lagoon. That's the way it works, and that's why the gates keep opening in the St. Lucie and San Sebastian Rivers, allowing millions of gallons of pesticide-filled muck into the Lagoon. I hate to say it, but all our complaining does is make a little ripple on the pond; we need a tsunami!"

"That's what I'm saying, Bob. A tsunami is exactly the sort of thing I'm talking about. We need a big bang, not a whimper; something so serious that everybody on the east coast of Florida will sit up and pay attention to."

"Shit, man, it sounds like you've got an idea that I'm not so sure is legal. Why don't you tell the rest of us what you're thinking?"

"Eco-terrorism. That's what we've got to do to bring attention to our once-beautiful water. If there's anybody interested in hearing my plan, you should stay. If you don't want to help us save our Lagoon, you should probably leave now."

Two men in the back got up to leave. Jack Baker saw them and spoke to them directly. "I understand you guys might not want to get involved in this discussion, but all of us formed this group to stop what's going on with the discharges. We all tried to do this the right way, but all we've seen from that is two years of aggravation and frustration. There's more dumping into the rivers now than there was before we got together. We're at a crossroads, guys. We either do something big or disband the group and watch our lagoon go further down the drain. That's where we are today; before you walk out of here you need to ask yourselves if you're okay with the Indian River Lagoon and the Seaway turning into one big septic tank for all the shit the government's allowing these bastards to dump. If you're not, and I don't think either of you are, you need to make the decision of your lifetime; are you in or out?"

The men paused as everyone else watched to see what they'd do. They all knew what Jack was talking about, but nobody in the room had ever dreamed it might come to something like this. But they also knew that Jack was right; it would take something more than another petition to make the politicos know how serious they were.

Both of the men who were about to leave returned to their seats. They heard what Jack had said and they knew he was right. Tom Brady, the older of the two, said 'listen, Jack, nobody here ever signed up to go to jail. We all wanted to do something that would make a difference, but eco-terrorism? Jesus, what the hell are you thinking about?"

Twelve eyes turned to Jack Baker, six men waiting to hear what he had to say.

"Everyone here should be familiar with the supply ships that run from Fort Pierce over to the Bahamas. They go back and forth carrying all sorts of supplies to the islands. It's how the Bahamas get most of their groceries and building supplies, and they leave our docks right here in Fort Pierce.

I have a friend who works down at the docks and he told me that about once a month the sugar factory out in Belle Glade ships a boatload of bulk sugar over to Nassau. They have a packaging plant near the commercial docks that packages the bulk sugar into everything from coffee packs to ten-pound bags, and they ship it all over the islands as a Bahamian product.

It's a very slick operation that they make a ton of money from. The regular monthly shipment leaves the dock next week on Tuesday. I say we have our own version of the Boston Tea Party."

"How would we do that, Jack? Will we dress up as Patriots and dump it into the Seaway?"

"No, Tom, that wouldn't be too good for the Turning Basin. We'd need to do something when the ship is out to sea. It would be pretty simple to attach an explosive device on the hull with a timer set to go off about 50 miles out. It would need to be a charge large enough to sink her, but small enough to give the crew plenty of time to evacuate the ship. There will be ample time for the Coast Guard to get out there to pull them out; there's only the Captain and four deckhands, so them getting off safely shouldn't be an issue."

"Holy Shit, Jack! Are you kidding me? A bomb on the hull? Who's going to do that?"

A tall, quiet man named Ken Lonergan stood up and said "I'm the one who'll plant the charge. I spent time with Seal Team 4 as a specialist in underwater demolition, and this job is a very simple maneuver. I can do this in my sleep, and nobody will get hurt, I promise you. Jack and I talked about this, and I think it's a helluva plan; I say let's do this!"

The five men who were out of the original loop stared back at Ken, then Jack. To a man, they couldn't believe that their little club would ever do something like this, but here it was, a plan that could work, one that could bring attention to the plight of their beloved Lagoon. Before thirty seconds had passed they all agreed to go forth with the operation; it was on!"

CHAPTER TWO

East of Fort Pierce, Florida
April 27, 2008

THE Nassau Queen had left the Fort Pierce docks a couple hours before at dawn; the captain had the ship on course, and the men sat around talking and smoking. There would be plenty to do once they got into Nassau, but the ride over was always enjoyable. It was a beautiful day, with cloudless, sapphire skies, and barely a breeze across the hull. The coffee was hot, and the men chewed on some breakfast sandwiches the cook had put together for them.

Each of the crewmen had chosen to make their living on the cargo boats of South Florida. Two of them were Haitians, hard working men who had left their impoverished island to make enough money to send home to their families in Port-au-Prince. Their once proud country, part of the island of Hispaniola, was now a barren wasteland, unlike the tropical jewel it had been in their youth. Many years of poverty had forced their people to cut down just about every tree in Haiti for building shacks and to burn for firewood. When the spring rains came, they would wash away layers of mud from the hills into the cities and villages. It was a cruel place to survive, and those who could, got out and settled elsewhere.

Lancelot Francois and Lamarrre St. Marie had found themselves a home in Fort Pierce. The city had become a haven for Haitian immigrants, so it was easy to settle in there. They had family and friends living on Avenue D, not far from the docks, and they each managed to rent a room close by. Avenue D was once the worst street in the city, home to rampant drug dealing and usage, and a never ending line of prostitutes, all willing to work for the crack they so desperately needed. But the city had cleaned it up, thanks to some Federal grants, and Avenue D had become a Haitian neighborhood. The men felt comfortable there.

Lancelot had found a job on the Nassau Queen the first week they arrived. The work on the ship was hard, but he liked the idea of being on the ocean most of the time. It was a break from the drudgery of so many hard labor jobs he had in Haiti; there, a man worked from sunrise to sunset for very little money, and he could never say there was anything left when he got done paying his bills. But here in America, he spent every day on the water, marveling at its beauty, and at the end of the week he had money left over to save. This money was going to be used to bring his wife and three children from Haiti to join him. He would have enough in the next couple of months; this kept him going every day.

Lamarre had been a cook for many years, working in hotels and restaurants around Port-au-Prince, but as the economy there turned sour, the jobs became very scarce. His last job had been as a fry cook in a Kentucky Fried Chicken restaurant. Kentucky Fried Chicken had dozens of restaurants throughout the Caribbean; some said it was the largest single chain of restaurants in all of the islands. Unfortunately, Lamarre had a grease accident, burning his right leg severely. Instead of helping him, the restaurant owner fired him for being stupid. He had often thought the owner was right; he was stupid for staying in Haiti!

He got a job working at the McDonald's on US 1, right near Seaway Drive. Two of his cousins worked there, and they had assisted him in finding work. After a few weeks, though, a position on the Nassau Queen opened up; it was a combination deck hand/cook position, and Lancelot made sure the Captain hired his friend. The two men were together on the seas; they couldn't have been happier.

Joshua Norton was a local man, born and raised in Fort Pierce. His family was part of a local legend known as the Highwaymen painters. The artists were all local black men who had been taught to paint landscapes by a prominent white artist named Bean Backus. Backus had taken a shine to his grandfather Howard and another man named Alfred Harris. Together they learned the basics of oil painting, and began to teach other black men in the area. Some of the new artists were friends, and some were family, and together they churned out hundreds of oil paintings that were sold along the local roads from the trunks of their cars.

You couldn't walk into a business, whether it was an attorney's office or a plumbing supply house, and not see one of their colorful paintings hanging on the walls. The paintings were framed in crown moldings they put together themselves, and the frames were painted white, with splashes of gold throughout. The art, once thought to be near worthless, was discovered in the late 90's and early 2000's and the prices rose meteorically. Paintings that sold for twenty-five dollars in 1975 started selling for several thousand dollars each, as collectors snapped them up wherever they could find them. His grandfather Howard, and his Uncle Robert, were two of the most talented of the early artists. Their works sold for outrageous sums; his father's brother Norman became a skilled painter in his own right and did very well selling his artwork.

Joshua, unfortunately, couldn't paint a barn with a twelve-inch brush, so he ended up working on the Nassau Queen. He was the First Mate, and he was in charge of the work load and the men. He'd made so many trips to the Bahamas over the years that he felt like the islands were his second home; one time, many years ago he had left the Queen to work on a ferry for the Albury's in Marsh Harbour, Abacos. He soon got tired of the short, tedious trips back and forth, same island to same island, over and over. When he heard the Queen was looking for a First Mate, he talked with the Captain, who didn't hesitate to hire him back. Joshua couldn't paint a barn, but he was one of the best boatmen he'd ever had on his ship.

The final crewmember was a newcomer, a local guy whose family had been around Fort Pierce for years. TW Parsons was the only white guy on the boat, but he didn't care. Like the others, he loved being on the water doing anything. He had pulled gill nets back when they were legal, and started crabbing after that. Rumor had it that he was a *Square Grouper* fisherman for a while, before the DEA really started hammering the local guys involved in the marijuana trade. A *square grouper* was a bale of marijuana sealed in plastic that was put overboard a big ship offshore, and retrieved by local fishermen. It had become the real treasure of the Treasure Coast for some time before the crackdown. It was said the grouper moved north to Brevard and Volusia Counties. The men on the Queen didn't care about his past; TW was one of them, just another brother on the water.

Captain Roland Brown was a local black man, like Joshua. His family had come to Fort Pierce before he was born to work on the farms and in the citrus groves. They were pickers mostly, and life had always been very difficult for them. His parents had six children, and he was the only boy. His father swore that his only son would do better than he ever did, and made it his life's mission to get Roland through school and into a better life. He died of cancer in Roland's last year of high school, never seeing his son walk down the aisle to get his diploma.

Roland had planned to go to the local community college after graduating, but he was heartsick over his father's death. School, for now, was out of the question, so he joined the US Coast Guard, and stayed in for eight years. When he got out he knew he wanted to be on the water, so he scored the First Mate's job on an old ferryboat, the Freeport Princess. When the Princess was lost at anchor during Hurricane Andrew in 1991, he was offered the Captain's position on a new boat, the Nassau Queen. He had now been at the helm of the Queen for seventeen years, and he had been thinking it was probably time to retire. He wanted Joshua to be his successor, the new Captain, so he had made Joshua take every Captain's course necessary to drive his boat. The young man was ready, he knew. What he didn't know was whether or not he was ready. "Time will tell, they say" he mused, as he drove the ship out into deep water.

Up on the bridge, the captain held his course. The wind had started picking up out of the southwest, but it wasn't enough to trouble his boat. While they had encountered mostly flat seas after dawn, the new wind was kicking up a three-to-four foot chop that wasn't unusual for this time of year. It was probably making it a little tougher for his crew to drink coffee, but that was certainly the worst of it.

He was right in his assessment. The splashing of sea water over the hull had forced the crew to move back off the bow, and into the small cabin they shared as a dining room and entertainment center. The entertainment was an old TV Capt. Brown had brought from home, along with a collection of DVD's nobody watched anymore. They had all seen most of the movies more than a few times, but the sound of the TV was relaxing as they sat around waiting to get into port. They were into their third pot of coffee, with The Godfather, Part II, playing on the TV, when they heard a very loud explosion on the starboard side of the ship.

The men jumped up and ran out onto the deck. There was heavy smoke coming out of what looked like a large hole in the right side of the hull; sea water seemed to be pouring into the hole, causing a loud hissing noise as the cold water hit the searing hot metal. The chop, once harmless, was slapping against the hull, driving more water in. The ship was already beginning to list to the starboard side; whatever caused the explosion was big enough to be a serious problem for the men on board.

Captain Brown came down from the bridge. "What the hell just happened? Did we get hit by something? I didn't see anything in the water, but that sure felt like a torpedo, or something like that, just hit us."

Distracted by the blast, the other men hadn't seen Joshua Norton stripping down and putting on snorkel gear. Before anyone realized it, he went over the rail into the water. The Captain and his men stood around, waiting for him to surface. When he did, his story put a chill into every one of them. "There's a horizontal tear in the hull that's probably twenty feet long by about four feet across. It's huge! It had to be explosives of some kind; the damage is beyond extensive, it's catastrophic! We're definitely going to need to get off this boat soon. There's no way it's not going under with all the weight we've got on board."

The Captain returned to the bridge and grabbed the radio. "Mayday! Mayday! Mayday! Coast Guard Station Fort Pierce, this is the Nassau Queen, out of Fort Pierce, en route to the Bahamas. We have just had an explosion in our hull that appears to be sabotage. I repeat, this is the Nassau Queen; we have had a major explosion on board that has seriously damaged the hull. We need immediate assistance; this ship is going down. There appears to be too much damage to keep her afloat. Do you copy, Fort Pierce?"

"Yes, Nassau Queen, we read you. We will send every available unit to your position asap. What are your coordinates?"

"Coast Guard Station Fort Pierce, my coordinates are 27*25'31.49"N – 79*52'26.05"W. Do you copy?"

"We copy Captain. Stay on the boat as long as you can. We'll have a helo and our big boat head your way in the next few minutes. They should be there within 15 minutes. Do you have a lifeboat on board?"

"We did, but it appears to have been blown off the boat in the blast. It's on the same side as the explosion; I'm guessing we lost it then. My men and I have life jackets, so we can go in if necessary."

"Alright, Captain. Hang in there; we'll be there shortly. Are you carrying any chemicals or toxic materials?"

"No, I've got a boatload of sugar, if you can believe that. Who the hell would blow up a ship full of sugar? It doesn't make any sense."

CHAPTER THREE

US Coast Guard Station, Fort Pierce, Florida

COMMANDER Rick Perry had heard the Mayday from his office. He leapt out of his chair and out onto the floor of the radio center, listening intently to the message from Capt. Brown. He knew Roland Brown personally, having met him years ago during an inspection of the Nassau Queen, and he knew that the Captain loved his ship and the men who crewed with him. He made a quick decision.

"Petty Officer, I'm flying the bird. Tell Ensign Williams to take command here for now, until we get back. That captain is a friend of mine; I want to get to him as soon as we can."

"Yes, sir, I'll forward your message to the ensign immediately. Go get'em, Commander!"

"I will, Petty Officer, you can take that to the bank!"

Commander Rick Perry had been grounded a few years back for something so bizarre it was hard to talk about. He had blown up a Coastie helo after he and two friends jumped out just before the blast, knocking the three of them into the water below like shells shot from a cannon. The fact that they all lived through the ordeal was truly a miracle, because the reason he incinerated the bird was to rid the world of a real-life demon, something he still had occasional nightmares over to this day. It all seemed like a bad dream now, but it was the scariest moment of his life, something he prayed would never happen again.

The Coast Guard issued a formal reprimand after *the incident*. He wasn't allowed to fly any Coast Guard helicopter or plane under any circumstances for a period of two years, and he was basically frozen in his rank as Commander of the Fort Pierce Station. What his superiors didn't know was that he loved the Fort Pierce Station; it was a terrific place to work. He had great fishing any night of the year right off the docks, and the weather was great. He suffered through the embarrassment quite well.

Together, with his old friends Captain Don Buckley and Pete Harris, he had spent countless hours chasing the big snook that roamed the docks at night. That was before *the incident*; the Captain had moved to the Bahamas with his wife Sue, and Pete had been killed by the monster they had buried at sea. It seemed like it was yesterday, but it had been almost four years since their nightmare. He missed Don and Pete whenever he went out on the docks to fish, but over time he had managed to move on. It hadn't been easy.

"*The incident*"; that's what the Coast Guard had called it, and he had accepted their terms. It could have been much worse; he had spent time in Vietnam during the war running patrol boats up the Mekong River, searching and rescuing, as they called it. Gunfire and rockets across the bow, and black body bags on deck, were everyday occurrences then, so being stuck in Fort Pierce was actually very pleasant.

But that was all behind him now; he had served his two-year suspension, and he was allowed to fly again. He still jumped at the chance to fly the search and rescue chopper that sat in his front yard, so every once in a while he took advantage of his rank and grabbed the stick of the big Sikorsky. He loved the power the helo generated and the speed at which it flew. Flying helicopters had been his dream job many years ago before he got moved along in the ranks, and it still got his juices flowing every time he flew one.

He grabbed his helmet as he flew out the door to the helo pad. The rescue crew was on board and ready to go, and the chopper was up and running. He jumped in the seat, strapped in and gave the order to take off. The Sikorsky effortlessly lifted itself off the pad and into the air as Commander Perry set a course due east, to the coordinates sent in by his friend. He saw the thirty-six foot power boat that had been confiscated from some drug runners a few years ago. With quad 200's on it, it was the fastest boat in their fleet, and now it sported the colors of the U.S. Coast Guard.

The big boat had been his friend Don's favorite when he served as the Station Chaplain, and the Captain couldn't resist taking the big blast boat out and letting it rip. Seeing the big powerboat running at full speed made him think that it was Don Buckley driving her, and not the Petty Officer at the wheel. The boat was already outside the Inlet entrance going like a bat out of hell. It was a beautiful sight!